Labrador Drift
A Cash Delaney Novel

BEVERLEE HUGHES

Published by Cliff Street Books

ISBN: 0692144064
ISBN-13: 978-0692144060
Library of Congress Control Number: 2018950331
Cover Photograph and Design by Joshua Adams
First Paperback Printing: July 2018
Printed in the United States of America

This one's for Garry and Debi Rust,
my delightful neighbors and friends.

"Life will break you. Nobody can protect you from that, and living alone won't either, for solitude will also break you with its yearning. You have to love. You have to feel. It is the reason you are here on earth. You are here to risk your heart. You are here to be swallowed up. And when it happens that you are broken, or betrayed, or left, or hurt, or death brushes near, let yourself sit by an apple tree and listen to the apples falling all around you in heaps, wasting their sweetness. Tell yourself you tasted as many as you could."

Louise Erdrich, *The Painted Drum*

"And what does anyone know about traitors, or why Judas did what he did?"

Jean Rhys, *Wide Sargasso Sea*

Labrador Drift

PROLOGUE

It was late June, a gorgeous Saturday afternoon in southeastern North Carolina, and we were enjoying a rather extravagant celebration because Junior Fisk, over the course of a year, had lost fifty pounds. That this considerable loss of weight was barely noticeable to any of the celebratory entourage except Junior did not matter in the least to him. He was ecstatic. So he had gone to the Fresh Market and purchased a bunch of stuff to eat and drink: tomato and avocado salad, boiled shrimp, two quarts of lobster meat, German potato salad, pickled beets, thick loaves of sourdough bread and a watermelon he'd infused with vodka that he claimed would, in his words, grow hair on a cue ball.

"I just ain't got the heart to tell him I don't for the life of me see it, Cash," Tallahassee Bodine said to me. "Lord knows I try. He's always turnin' this way and that, but I absolutely do not see no difference." I chuckled, but I knew what he meant.

"Nobody sees it but Junior," Stella Conroy said to him. "The man is five feet six and weighs three hundred and fifty pounds, Tally. He looks just like he did when he weighed four hundred, for Christ's sake."

Tally is Junior's best friend and together they resemble Jack Sprat and his wife, because Tally is over six feet tall and skinny as a rail. Add to that contrast the fact that Tally's skin is as dark as a piece of anthracite and Junior's is as white as a lily, and the picture of these two polar opposites is complete.

The three of us were lounging on the port deck of the Portofino, Jefferson Davis's fifty-foot Sea Ray, which he'd anchored a good distance offshore from the marina at Southport. We were sitting a fair distance from the inner edge of the Labrador Current, the north/south cold rush of the Atlantic that runs inside the opposing flow of the warm Gulf Stream. Jeff and Cooper Grey were sport fishing somewhere on the aft deck of the boat. Stella and Tally and I were drinking vodka and tonic and eating ice cold shrimp with lemon chunks and Calabash hot cocktail sauce. Junior was riding an enormous inner tube tied to the rear of the boat. Every once in awhile, we could hear him singing his version of "Midnight Special." He was so off key it barely resembled music, but nobody minded. We were all enjoying ourselves and the ocean was as calm as it gets; it resembled rippled glass.

"You're turning red," Stella said to me. "Y'all need some of that coconut oil. You absolutely do not want to burn in this hot sun." She was wearing a form fitting black swimsuit and was already brown as a berry.

"I'm drowning in coconut oil right now," I said to her. "Besides, I always burn a bit before I brown. And in this outfit, I'm not that exposed." I had on a pair of red Bermuda shorts topped by a yellow polo shirt.

"You burn too much, you blister, you peel," Stella countered.

"She ain't never gonna brown like you, Stella," Tally said to her. "She don't have your colorin'." Stella is a natural blond. I'm brunette.

"Whoa," Jefferson Davis shouted, interrupting this discussion of my melatonin. "Hang on. Don't let any slack in the line." His voice carried from wherever he was standing on the other side of the boat.

"I got it," Cooper Grey said to him. He sounded excited.

"Don't lose it. Don't force it; let it run. Jesus, it's a monster. You got a heavy enough line on that reel?"

"Too late to worry about that now," Coop said. "Here he comes; he's running right straight at us."

"Tighten up that slack; he'll tire tryin' to fight you and the boat."

"You better grab your biggest net," Cooper said to him.

"Net hell," Jeff said. "Katherine," he hollered, "we are goin' to need you over here right now."

"Let's go rescue our boys," Stella said to me, draining her drink and popping a shrimp in her mouth. In her case, Cooper is her husband, and she'd married him twice to prove it. In my

case, Jefferson is my significant other which is an ungodly awkward way of saying he's the man I am currently spending time with. These arrangements suit the four of us, more or less, from one day to the next.

I felt so lazy I could barely get up enough energy to move.

"It's a cobia," Coop said at the top of his lungs. "It's forty pounds if it's an ounce. We need you now."

Although I had no idea what a cobia was, I stood up quickly and followed Stella. When we reached them, Cooper was leaning way back in an unsecured deck chair and straining against the strength of the fish; Jeff was hanging off the side of the railing at an angle that looked precarious to me. Only one of his feet was still touching the hard surface of the walkway.

I grabbed the back of his swim trunks, braced myself against the decking, and held on. Stella had managed to wrap one hand around the reel. It looked to me as though the fish was winning.

"Can you reach him," Coop said to Jefferson. "I'm really running out of steam."

"Give me a little more leeway, Katherine, quick," Jeff said to me.

"I give you a little more and you'll be swimming for shore," I said, but I loosened my grip a tiny bit.

The fish was hurtling itself against the boat and Stella now had both of her hands above Cooper's on the rod, which was bent at an angle that resembled an upside down capital U. All of a sudden, Jeff pulled both of his arms back and swung hard, which planted the gaff he was holding deep in the high middle of the cobia's back. The giant fish was hooked and the thrashing diminished while the water turned red. It was such a sudden loss of tension that Cooper tumbled out of his chair and Stella staggered backwards, still holding the rod.

"I ain't seen a fish that big since before my mama could vote," Tallahassee Bodine said. He'd been standing a few feet off, watching the drama unfold. "We always called them lemonfish when I was a child and boy they are some good eats."

"Help me lift it into the boat," Jeff said to me. He was breathing heavily.

"Is it dead?" I asked. I am not enamored of the basics of fishing.

"Not quite. We get it landed, it will be." All four of us managed to hoist it onto the aft deck. The huge fish flopped around until Jefferson walloped it over the head with a hammer.

"Now it's dead," he said. He was sweating and grinning from ear to ear.

"Grab my camera from that table over there," Cooper said to Stella. "I want to remember this bruiser. He's a personal best."

"We gotta weigh and measure it," Jeff said, as Stella snapped some photos with the phone.

"I am gonna send some of these to daddy," Stella said. Her father, Billy Conroy, is the Sheriff of Brunswick County. This is a bonus to Stella and me because he sometimes helps us in any private investigations we are hired to do. "He will be an extremely jealous man."

Weighed and measured, the cobia was an astounding 42 inches long and 61 pounds, and all three of the boys had already started to clean and gut it when we heard a heart stopping scream emanate from the rear of the boat.

"Junior's in trouble," I said to Stella.

When we got to the small rear landing deck and looked, Junior was out of his inner tube, which was nowhere in sight, and he was flailing around wildly. He was barely being kept afloat by the waterproof vest he was wearing. He was also hysterical.

"Don't thrash, Junior." Stella yelled to him. "Calm yourself." Then she said quietly to me, "Throw him something before he sinks. Neither one of us could keep him afloat, get him back to the boat. He can't swim good and we'd drown tryin' to save him."

I unhooked a life preserver and tossed it to him. He grabbed at it and missed, which pushed it out of his reach. Stella looked at me. "He's gonna go under, we don't reach him soon. That vest cannot protect him much longer."

I nodded and reeled in the lifeline to try again. My second throw worked like a perfect pitch in a game of horseshoes. I hit the jackpot and the life preserver settled in over his head. The man was safe for the moment.

"Where in hell is your inner tube, Junior," I said to him.

"Around left," he said, pointing right. He was sucking in huge gulps of air. "I got trajectored right out of it. Y'all think I would choose to go without true safety in the Atlantic Ocean? I am not an imbecile." His swim trunks were ballooning below him like a multi-colored flower garden.

I glanced at Stella. "Trajectored?" I said.

Stella gave me a shrug. "Y'all know he massacres words," she said. "Go look, see what the hell he's talkin' about. I'll haul him in."

When I walked to my left and looked down, there was the inner tube. The rope that had secured it to the boat was frayed and floating in a circle around it. But it was what was floating in it that left me slack-jawed and totally confounded.

"Stella," I said in a voice that sounded tight and high and loud even to me.

"I am on my way," she hollered.

"This is not good," I was muttering when she walked up beside me. "This is not good at all."

"Well fuck," Stella said. "What in this world has happened here?"

"I have no idea," I said to her. "But you'd better notify your father. We've got to get this mess ashore."

"That may require some original thinking," she said.

Being kept afloat by Junior's inner tube was a corpse that was missing one of its arms from the elbow down and half of its face. An assortment of ragged clothes was hanging off what was left of the body. Something had eaten the flesh of the jaw and half the cheeks, along with most of the nose. Two empty eye sockets were staring up at us and a silly-looking variegated tie looked to be strangling the already broken neck. Ribbons of seaweed crowned the nearly bald head. The most that could be said was that whoever it had been in life was male and maybe middle-aged.

And that was what we could see. It was what we couldn't see that would ultimately bring a tidal wave of trouble to these peaceful southern shores.

CHAPTER ONE

"Tell me in detail just what is distressin' y'all," Sheriff Billy Conroy said to the man sitting across from him in his office in Bolivia, North Carolina. The man had called earlier requesting to meet with the Sheriff. "I need to see am I understanding you correctly."

"My wife and I believe that someone is trying to sabotage our vineyard," the man, whose name was Paul Sargasso, said. He was a well-dressed man in his forties of a certain Mediterranean lineage, built close to the ground and sturdy. He might have been a wrestler in his youth.

"Uh huh," the Sheriff said. "And your vineyard is where?"

"We own four hundred and seventy acres outside Little Prong," the man said. "Only a hundred and fifty of those acres are currently tillable and suitable for grapes. The rest is a mixture of woods, pastures, and the odd designated site, by which I mean a small cemetery and an old homestead."

"Little Prong," Billy Conroy said to him. "There's what, a hundred souls livin' around and about that so called populated place?"

"We don't suspect it's any of our neighbors," Sargasso said. "Most of them work for us at picking time. We pay them well. There is mutual respect that has been created and everyone in the area appreciates and nurtures it."

"So who is it you suspect?" the Sheriff said, taking note of the man's precise use of the English language along with his accent, which was definitely northern.

"We don't know. That's why I came to talk with you. But we've seen too many of our muscats irreparably damaged to simply put it down to coincidence. There's got to be some foul play involved."

Billy Conroy considered this. I don't know squat about growin' grapes, he thought to himself. Then he glanced at his cell phone, which was displaying a picture of a cobia that had just been caught by his son-in-law on a boat where he should have been a major part of the action, not to say the angler himself. He prided himself on his expertise when it came to landing the big fish. The Sheriff, feeling more than a little disgruntled, forced himself to look away.

"You say sabotaged, what are y'all implyin'?" Billy said to the man.

"Broken vines, an occasional stripping of grapes," Sargasso said. "Last week four whole rows of newly planted seedlings were ripped completely out of the soil and tossed helter skelter. None of them could be saved."

"Deer or varmints couldn't have done all that?" the Sheriff asked him.

"We thought so at first. For awhile, we were satisfied to conclude the deer were to blame, especially for the stripping. But these uprooted vines could only have happened at the hand of humans. We need your help, Sheriff Conroy."

Billy Conroy sighed deeply. He was responsible for the welfare of the populace of a good sized county in North Carolina and his resources were severely limited. In this southern state, public resources were always limited due to the current controlling legislators who might as well have had Marie Antoinette's slogan regarding the general population's wellbeing tattooed on their behinds: "Let them eat cake." The Sheriff often thought that most probably some of them did.

"I will look into it," he said.

"What does that mean, sir," Paul Sargasso said, standing up so suddenly his chair fell backwards behind him.

Billy Conroy slowly stood up. His six-foot-four, well-muscled body dwarfed the other man, whose wide green eyes behind a pair of frameless lenses were nevertheless regarding him with suspicion. "I can't exactly say, Mr. Sargasso," he said to the man. "But rest assured, I am registerin' your concern and I will investigate. Whatever is goin' on over there, we will determine and deal with in good time. Please leave your address and phone number with my assistant Louise Dickson on your way out."

Five minutes later, while he was pouring himself a cup of his special blended coffee, Louise knocked on his door.

"Come on in," he said. "Pour yourself a cup, Louise. And then tell me what, if anything, we know about Little Prong."

"Well," Louise said, looking at him with a straight face, "we're pretty sure it's not a tuning fork Billy."

Billy Conroy stared at her. Then he said "You'd best thank your stars I swallowed that mouthful of hot coffee right before you hit me with such sass." Then he grinned.

"It's just another way of saying that really we don't know anything. It's perfectly possible there's never been a single crime committed over there. Well, not in the past seventy five years at least."

"So we are gonna be dancin' in the dark," he said.

"Again," Louise said. "Who do you want to send to take a look? Lloyd Harris? He's bright enough."

"He's also a hothead. He tossed my son-in-law in jail a while ago despite the man's reasonable explanation of what had happened. We can't be relyin' on guys who act before they think," the Sheriff said to her.

Louise Dickson smiled benevolently at him before she said, "That might have been a perfect description of you, Billy, thirty years ago. And look where you are today."

The Sheriff contemplated his coffee cup before responding. Finally, in a moment of concession, he simply said, "Is there a reason why I haven't asked you to marry me?"

"Not one that I can think of," she said evenly, "unless it's your possible aversion to the possibility that I might say no." Billy Conroy looked at his longtime assistant and realized she was right. He did love her and was reluctant to admit that love because, well, why? She was a striking looking woman, tall and slender, full of grace with long salt and pepper hair that she often wore loose and wavy around her face. He often simply sat behind his desk and admired her as she moved about the office. Maybe I am afraid she'll say no, he thought to himself. And maybe she actually would.

The loud ringtone of his cell phone startled them both. He looked at the number. "It's Stella," he said.

When he answered the call, his daughter said, "We've got a decomposing corpse stuck in an inner tube we need to get to shore, daddy."

"Say what?" the Sheriff exclaimed.

"A dead man, daddy, inhabitin' Junior Fisk's inner tube. The damn thing came up from below, torpedoed Junior right out of it. He very nearly drowned; would have if Cash hadn't reached him with a life preserver."

"I thought y'all were fishin', havin' a party," her father said, trying to digest this information. "Now you're dealin' with a corpse?" Louise looked at Billy with alarm.

"Yes," Stella said. "And this is one we do not know what to do with. From what we can see, half the face is gone and one of the arms to the elbow. We don't know what's goin' on that we can't see. For all we know the damned thing could be set to explode, somebody messes with it."

Billy Conroy ran through his options before he said to his daughter, "All right. Can you stabilize the scene for an hour?"

"I reckon," Stella said. "Unless a storm suddenly decides to materialize, which at the moment seems highly unlikely."

Billy Conroy put his hand over his cell phone. "Call Lloyd Harris at home," he said to Louise. "Tell him to bring his diving gear and meet me at the main pier in Southport. We gotta figure out how to get a decomposing corpse to shore without we cause significantly more damage.

And Louise," the Sheriff added, "give me an hour and then notify the Coast Guard over on Oak Island what we're dealin' with; make it a courtesy call. Tell them the details will follow. I don't want them gettin' in an uproar over this, not this time of year, y'all get my drift."

Louise Dickson nodded. She knew exactly what he meant: there was no good reason to upset the tourists who were streaming into area beaches by the hundreds every hour of every day, from now until the end of September. "Maybe I'll just send a general text message alerting them to a fait accompli," she said as she walked out the door. "Otherwise, that chatty Cathy over there who's always manning the phone will want a detailed explanation."

"Good idea," Billy said. "Blind cc me, okay Louise?"

"Don't I always, Billy," she said and winked at him over her shoulder.

CHAPTER TWO

"Well, Billy," the Medical Examiner from Onslow Memorial Hospital on call for Brunswick County said, "your fellow drowned, and that's about as much as I'm prepared to say at this time."

"Meanin' what, Don?" the Sheriff said.

"Meanin' I can't tell you one way or another if his neck was snapped by human hands, the motion of the ocean, a log he collided with, or what," Donald Payson said with obvious annoyance in his voice." There's too much physical erosion present. But his lungs are holdin' seawater, which says he was still breathin' when he landed in the Atlantic. Chances are that's all we'll ever know. I'm inclined to rule it accidental or, I suppose, undetermined."

We were standing in a good-sized room that was painted an antiseptic yellow and encouraged claustrophobia; I knew that his annoyance had nothing to do with this current situation. Rather, he was disgruntled because a Republican legislator from Brunswick County had done away with the Brunswick County Coroner's Office, one that had been open for decades; and this meant that the workload now fell on members of the hospital's medical staff.

I glanced at Stella, who was humming an unrecognizable tune and tapping her left foot to some internal beat. The air felt thick and very, very heavy. I was finding it difficult to breathe. And there were two other tables to our left where corpses were sheet-covered. I didn't know whether they'd been autopsied or not, and I didn't care one way or another. The sheer sterility of the room was monumentally oppressive. I couldn't imagine how people could find it in themselves to work in such a place.

"Okay," Billy Conroy said. "Well, at least we know who he is, and it ain't a name I am in any way familiar with."

"What is the name again," the Medical Examiner said.

The Sheriff turned to me. I was still trying to breathe. Death has a particular, peculiar odor no matter how you might try to disperse it and it has to do with an awful sweet stench that seems to invade your nose and settle there whenever you encounter it. All I was craving was a long, hot shower. I looked at the small piece of indestructible plastic in my hand.

"His name is Woodrow Keats," I said. "That's all we could find when we searched the body."

"No," said Donald Payson. "He's no one I know, either. It sounds as though he might be a tourist and that's not really copasetic, Billy; not this time of year in particular."

The dead man's empty eye sockets were pointing directly at the hot light shining down on what was left of him while I watched a small sea worm sidle out of his half-eaten jaw. I tried not to gag.

"Y'all don't have to tell me," the Sheriff said. "I've got Louise lookin' into him even as we speak. With luck he'll turn out to have tumbled into the ocean way north of the Outer Banks and I can hand him over to some other jurisdiction. Send me a copy of your report once you sign off on it. And Don, in my book, accidental beats undetermined every day of the week"

"I've got to get out of here," I said quietly to Stella. "Right now."

"Let's go," Stella mouthed as she grabbed my elbow and hustled me out of the room. When we reentered the daylight, the sun seemed hundreds of times brighter than it had been and I found myself blinking furiously against the glare until I nearly stumbled up against a short, rather plump very attractive woman dressed in a black pantsuit. Two men in complementary grey business suits stood on either side of her.

"Yes?" I said to her. Stella was humming tunelessly again. You'd have thought it was a clue of some sort. But it wasn't. It was nerves.

"What are you two doing here on a Saturday," the woman said curtly. "And who are you?"

"Why?" I answered.

As though I hadn't spoken, the agitated woman looked to her left and said to the guy standing nearly at attention, "Why in god's name haven't we surrounded this place by now, kept it off limits to civilians?"

"Beatrice," the guy said softly. "Consider. They are obviously just two American girls."

"Means nothing these days," she snapped. "Again, who are you," she said to me.

"We are two American girls who are just leavin'" said Stella in her thickest mush-mouthed southern drawl. "We thought the floater in there might could be our cousin Big Orville; he went fishin' Tuesday last and upped and vanished. But it ain't him. So we are goin' home. Y'all gonna be developin' a massive migraine over that, lady? Or are y'all here about the Big O yourself."

I bit my tongue nearly in half to keep from laughing out loud.

"What," the woman in black said to the other guy, who was

actually smiling, "did she just say?"

"They were, I think, looking for their lost cousin Orbit or Orson or some such; but anyway, they are now leaving, having been unable to locate him here," the guy explained patiently. "Have a nice day, ladies," he said as he steered the woman around us and proceeded to the front door of the morgue. Stella and I didn't exactly take off running to her car, but we certainly didn't linger.

"Feds of some sort," I said to her as we drove out of the lot. "I wonder what in hell is really going on."

"I have no earthly idea," she said. "And I am far from certain that I want to know. I just hope neither one of us comes up when the three of them powwow with daddy. Dealin' with feds in this day and age is a true nightmare."

"Well," I said, "if he's important enough to bring them here, it's going to be a mess whether we like it or not."

Stella looked quickly at me. "Shit," she said to no one. Then she spoke a number into her dashboard telephone technology. A ringtone sounded.

"Conroy," said her father.

"Go outside, daddy," she said.

After a few seconds of empty air, we heard Billy say, "Excuse me for a minute, folks." Stella was humming again. Then the Sheriff said, "Listen Stella, three federal agents are here. My guess Homeland Security, but they could be FBI or even CIA. I can't be messin' around. This is obviously somethin' damned serious. What is it y'all want?"

"Cash and I do not want to be involved in it, whatever it is, y'all get my drift."

"Nobody's gonna involve you," he said. "The corpse bumped into a boat. I got called. I retrieved the body. End of story, Stella."

"None of those suits mentioned us, they got to the morgue?"

"That's right," Billy said. "Now listen, Louise, y'all get me that information, you hear? I'll get up with you later today." And with that, Billy Conroy disconnected.

"He had company there at the end," I said to Stella.

"Uh huh," she said. "Whaddya think about askin' Sarah to research this character Keats?"

"Depends whether or not she'd leave a trail for some federal cyber sleuth to follow," I said. "We sure as hell don't want to compromise Sarah's ability to operate under the radar. It's her best asset."

"She's hacked the government a time or two," Stella said. "Just last year, that job we did for Corning."

"Unclassified information," I said. "This thing doesn't sound unclassified to me. But we can see what she says. She's over at Mickey's for the day. Said she'd be home tomorrow sometime."

In a nutshell, Sarah Ehrenson is a computer genius/information anthropologist with a PhD in political science from Georgetown University. She can find out anything about anything, anyone, anywhere, any time; and she works with Stella and me in our private investigations business. She is also my best friend. We share a house in Carolina Beach that she is still trying to persuade the owner to sell to us. After three years of trying, she remains unsuccessful but hopeful. That's Sarah. She never gives up. Mickey is Michael L.L. Huntley, Esquire, a highly successful defense attorney and Sarah's life partner.

"Well," Stella said, "tomorrow is soon enough. My curiosity may be piqued, but I am still not wantin' to get dragged into this, whatever it turns out to be. You goin' to Jeff's boat or home?"

"Home," I said. "I need a shower."

The ringtone that burst forth from her dashboard phone startled us both.

"Can y'all take that," Stella said. She was driving her usual eighty miles an hour, which requires her full attention. "It's voice activated. Just aim yourself at it."

"Hello."

"Cash?" said a voice I'd heard before.

"Yep."

"Billy told me to call you and Stella. It's about that corpse y'all ran into," Louise Dickson said.

"Okay," I said.

"Woodrow Keats is a highly respected recruiter for the CIA, a twenty-year man. The last time they could account for his whereabouts, he was interviewing marines at Fort Lejeune, and they are profoundly unhappy to learn of his body floating off our shoreline. Billy is, to say the very least, equally unhappy about this situation. He says to tell y'all he'll probably need your help after all, whether you like it or not, if he decides he needs to investigate. Deep background only. And Cash," she said, "for what it's worth, he says to tell you he's sorry. But nevertheless, there it is."

Stella slammed her right hand against the Mustang's steering wheel and nearly sent us flying into the ditch on the side of the road.

"Damn it to hell!!" she said vehemently. "Accidental death my ass!"

I looked at her. We both knew what neither one of us chose to say out loud. Woodrow Keats had probably been murdered. Whether or not anyone would ever be able to prove it was completely irrelevant. The CIA was in town. If need be, it created proof.

CHAPTER THREE

Cassandra Quick sat quietly on the gallery of her small home in Elrod, North Carolina, rocking in a chair she'd made herself, and thought about her most recent surveillance of the land that now was owned by a man whose last name was Sargasso. Lifetimes ago, before the assent and conquest of the white man, it had been part of a tract of land settled by a bunch of Lumbee Indians, some of whom were her ancestors. She smiled to herself at the patchwork quilt of her genealogy. I am as much Caucasian as Indian, she thought. I am even a small dollop African American. But in my heart, I am Indian; it is the spiritual well that quenches my deepest roots.

Anyone who eventually met her would have disagreed with her chosen ethnicity, and that was fine with Cassandra. She was a woman of significant presence with smooth, silky skin the color of old bone; startling, thick long blond hair she often wore in braids and unexpected pale green eyes, not unlike certain shades of apple jade. Although she was not tall, those who met her described her as such and later could not account for their mistaken impression. "Magic" was often Cassandra's explanation. It was never said in jest, although mostly she allowed a smile to accompany it. Best to keep the hounds at bay, she reckoned.

And her house was her sanctuary, one she had designed and built herself. It was one large room with interior walls covered in refinished shiplap boards she had scavenged from various old barns around the countryside. And there was a kitchen at the far end, of which she was particularly proud. It boasted both a full-sized refrigerator and a small sideboard freezer where she stored the fish and rabbits and squirrels she always caught in summer that provided good food all winter. Her cook stove was ideal for the kinds of dinners she preferred: it was a six burner wood stove that she'd found in an abandoned shack several miles from where she was now sitting. She'd cleaned and polished it and returned it to its former glory and it rewarded her every time she used it. Cassandra was well-known around Elrod for her delicious gourmet dinners. The home also boasted a full bath and a large bedroom. To Cassandra, it was a mansion and she loved it and cherished it, her beautiful home on the hill.

An old blue pickup truck lumbered into view, raising clouds of dust from the dry dirt road that led to her home. It pulled alongside her gallery and parked, and a tall, deeply tanned and thin man with a shaved head, wearing flip flops, old blue jeans and a black tee shirt that read, "If I agreed with you we both would be wrong" got out. It was Cassandra's cousin on her Lumbee mother's side, Cudworth Sweat. People who knew him called him Cuddy. People who really knew him called him Chief.

"I'm parched," he said, walking up the few steps to the gallery.

"Beer's cold," Cassandra said. "Grab a couple. Then come sit."

As he settled into the chair beside her and handed her a bottle of beer, Cuddy said laconically, "He went to the Sheriff's place today. Musta called ahead 'cause Billy and the woman were both there."

"Who confirmed?" she said.

"Me," he said. "I followed him."

"So he's stewin'," Cassandra said, taking a long swig of beer.

"I'd say so. He looked mad as any worker bee I've ever seen defendin' his hive when he left. Peeled outta there like a man possessed."

"Well," she said, a grin creasing her face, "we don't really know what he was mad about. If he was askin' for help from the law, it couldda been Billy Conroy. You know the impression that man can give to some people. But Sargasso is possessed. He just don't comprehend it quite yet. Next time, we'll leave him something he thinks is a clue."

"You decided what?" Cuddy asked.

"Pretty much," she said, draining her bottle of beer. "Damn that's a fine thirst quencher. Let's have another."

When they were enjoying their second beer, Cassandra said, "I think if I leave a trail of footprints where I destroy a few more vines, it'll startle him. I need to be able to gauge his true temperament: what's his reaction? What does it drive him to do?"

Cuddy Sweat nodded. "I like it," he said. "I like it a whole bunch. When you goin' back?"

"Couple three days," she said. "I want to give him time to convince himself that really he's safe and comfy in his private cocoon—that his concern's all in his head. Though he don't recognize it for what it is, he's got guilt corroding his heart. And his money is the temporary medicine that eases it. But once I drag him outside the universe of his own mind, and keep him there, he's mine, Cuddy."

"Ours, Cassandra," her cousin said softly. "He's ours."

I woke up late on Sunday morning. What I saw first was blazing sunlight streaking through my curtains; what I heard first was Dinah Washington singing "What a Difference a Day Makes"; and what I smelled first was bacon. Two things occurred to me: I needed a shower and I was starving. The first I could handle in ten minutes. The second could well be a long, drawn out affair with bacon sandwiches on sourdough and scrambled eggs with cheese and scallions and mushrooms and hot hazelnut coffee with sugar and real cream. My mouth started to water. It was going to be a fabulous day and to hell with the CIA.

When I walked into the kitchen to pour a cup of coffee, Sarah was leaning against the side counter wearing ivory lounging pajamas and drinking what looked to be a bloody mary. Her deep red hair was a bit messy and I idly wondered how many drinks she'd consumed.

"A tad early for you isn't it," I said to her.

"It's twelve thirty," she said, chomping on a big stalk of celery. "And anyhow, I've been working since eight this morning."

"Doing what?"

"The usual. Stella called me on my way home from Mickey's, asked me to research a guy named Woodrow Keats, whose corpse she said bumped into the Portofino yesterday and interrupted your little Weight Watchers party. She said to keep it under the radar and away from snoops, seeing as how he is a celebrated albeit deceased CIA Grand Poobah."

"So you did the research?" I asked.

"I did indeed," she said and finished off her mixed drink. "You want a bacon sandwich on sourdough? Or there's fresh lox and some sesame bagels. Cream cheese, too."

I stared at her. I was quickly losing my appetite. "Woodrow Keats," I said. "The rundown, Sarah. Please."

"Well, it wasn't the easiest hacking I've ever done, but it was probably the best. If they are extremely lucky they may discover who I was when I visited their site about twenty years after I'm dead."

I sighed. Deeply. I know she loves to play with my store of patience. She always has. "Sarah, who is—was, Mr. Keats?"

"A recruiter for the CIA," she said.

"I know that already," I said testily, noticing my voice begin to rise. "Louise told us that much yesterday afternoon. Is that all there is?"

"No," she said and looked away from me. She was rinsing out her glass in the sink. "He is actually very special. In point of fact, he is the one and only recruiter for a deeply clandestine operation of the CIA; sort of their version of a navy seal unit, but even deeper. This particular area of espionage activity is so top secret that the agency itself formally refuses to admit its existence. It's deniability squared. I doubt even the so-called President knows anything about it, for which, of course, we should be eternally grateful. Just reading what little information there is on the site made me quite nervous and you know very well I do not suffer from paranoia."

I felt my right hand go ice cold and begin to quiver, so I quickly put my coffee cup down before I dropped it. Sarah glanced at my trembling hand.

"Why are you shaking," she said, sounding somewhat alarmed. "You've got nothing to do with this. Stella is just being nosy."

"That's true as far as it goes but it's not exactly the entire picture," I said.

Sarah turned and looked me straight in the eye. "Tell me," she said.

"Well," I said, "as we were leaving the morgue, we sort of lied to the folks from the CIA who showed up to investigate the guy's death," I said.

"You what?" Sarah said loudly. "Why in hell would you do that?"

"We didn't want to be involved," I said. I sounded sheepish even to myself.

Thankfully, the noise of the front door opening and closing broke the tension of the moment.

"Sarah bring y'all up to speed?" Stella Conroy said. She was wearing white shorts and a pink halter and her long blond hair was pulled back in a ponytail. She didn't sound at all happy. I nodded. "Well, it's a right fine pile of cow poop we stepped into," she said. "You think those suits'll find their way to our door, poke around, make mountains out of molehills, bother the living hell right out of us?"

"I don't know," I said. "Probably. We need to talk to your father, see what he told them. See what they told him."

"If they told him anything," Sarah said, sounding somewhat mollified. "This probably goes way beyond the pay grade of the people initially sent to investigate."

"They knew it was important enough to restrict civilian access to the morgue," I said.

I heard a delicate slurping sound behind my back and when I turned to look, there was Minerva, our domineering calico cat named for the Roman Goddess of Wisdom and War, who chose to live with us when we first moved to the island. She was drinking happily from my now nearly empty cup of coffee and cream. Sarah saw her at the same time I did and swatted at her.

"Jesus Christ, Minerva," Sarah said impatiently, grabbing the cup away from her. "Now you'll have the runs all day long. Let her out of the house," she said to Stella.

"Why don't y'all decide to go play in the traffic," Stella muttered as she maneuvered the cat toward the door. "We're lucky, something might hit you."

Minerva stopped short and glared. Then she let loose with one of her horrific brain-splitting yowls. I swear she could raise the dead. It seemed a perfect precursor to whatever lay ahead for all of us.

CHAPTER FOUR

Brooke Malanga stood in the front hallway of her oceanfront cottage at Topsail Beach, North Carolina and stared at the postcard in her hand. It was early on Monday morning and she had just collected her mail from Saturday. The front of the postcard showed a massive display of wildflowers that could be thriving anywhere the sun shined. The message side of the card contained just two block printed words: "REMEMBER IVANHOE". There was no signature. She wouldn't usually have concerned herself with small mysteries such as this because she was disinclined to ponder the vagaries of the universe. A year ago, she'd have tossed it out and forgotten about it. Today, she placed it on a side table she kept in her foyer for incidentals and walked into her kitchen to pour herself a cup of tea and think about it.

Her kitchen overlooked the ocean and boasted a large picture window that provided her with a magnificent view of the Atlantic, which was one of the things she treasured most about her home. The day was nearly cloudless, with a sky that boasted several shades of blue and sunlight that bathed the white sand beach with a golden touch she never tired of. Her tea leaves had been steaming for ten minutes in the four-cup pot she preferred. Today she had steeped a delicate white tea, which she appreciated for its subtlety, complexity and natural sweetness. Brooke Malanga sighed deeply as she poured a cup of the tea and carried it to a small window seat where she sat and contemplated how to go about locating her younger brother Eric. He was, after all, her only living (if he was still living) relative. And she owed him nothing less than to find him and help him in any way that she could.

Ten months ago, Eric had officially gone missing, and ever since she'd begun to pay attention to small things such as this postcard with its two-word greeting that was lying on her foyer table. Could it be a message from her brother? And if so, what was he telling her? Or was he, as the Central Intelligence Agency refused to deny or acknowledge, dead? Not only was he neither dead nor alive to that agency, he had not worked within their ranks at all, according to the official statement she had received from that organization upon inquiry. This she knew to be a lie. Her brother had told her as much shortly before he left America for points unknown, overseas. But challenging the CIA was akin to challenging Goliath without a slingshot. She had gotten nowhere.

Was Eric alive? This was the question she posed over and over to herself without a clear idea of how to answer it. And now this card: "Remember Ivanhoe." The words meant nothing to her. She took a deep breath and walked to her bedroom to collect her phone just as it rang.

"This is Brooke," she said. She never said "Hello."

"Ms. Malanga, this is Beatrice Bush."

"Yes?"

"I'm wondering if we might meet later this morning," Beatrice said.

"Regarding what?" she asked.

"It's regarding your brother Eric," the woman said.

"What is your affiliation," Brooke Malanga said, suddenly tense, "that would give you any knowledge whatsoever of my brother."

Beatrice Bush paused. Then she said reluctantly, "I'm with the federal government, Ms. Malanga. Believe me when I say we need to talk. But we can't continue this conversation over an unsecured line. If you can meet me in two hours at the Coast Guard Station at Wrightsville Beach, I would appreciate it. When you get to the main gate, ask for me. Someone will bring you to where I'm located. Can you do that?"

Brooke Malanga experienced two things at once: her heart and her thoughts nearly raced away from her. She struggled to bring her voice under control. Finally, she said in a remarkably steady cadence, "Yes. I can do that."

"Fine. I'll see you then," said Beatrice Bush. "And thank you," she added as she broke the connection.

The minute she ended the call, Brooke walked quickly back to her foyer, grabbed the postcard, took it to the kitchen, reached for a kitchen match, struck it and watched the postcard turn to ash which she blew into her kitchen sink and rinsed away. She had her answer, regardless of how inadvertently it had arrived. Her brother Eric was alive. But Brooke Malanga had no intention of helping the Central Intelligence Agency prove it.

"A polite white man in a grey suit stopped by the house this morning," Tallahassee Bodine said to Stella and me. "I ain't exactly happy 'bout it, though. He was a nosy parker, but I couldn't really say what was drivin' his curiosity. I did my best to convince him I was as dumb as he thought I outta be, y'all get my meanin'. Told him I was asleep in the sun when Billy took possession of that corpse. I ain't want to say he believed me, one way or another. Is somethin' goin' on? Is it anythin' we need worry about? If so, I got to warn Junior and him and me'll take a trip to Myrtle Beach, play some cards, wait for whatever it is to blow over."

"What is goin' on is a bunch of bullshit," Stella said to him. "But it's federal bullshit and I really stepped full-bore in it."

We were sitting in the private back room of our investigations' office on Lake Park Boulevard in Carolina Beach late on Monday morning.

"The dead guy," I said to Tally, "was an important recruiter for the CIA. Stella and I chose to avert questioning from them by implying we had nothing to do with recovering the body. The fib is coming back to haunt us."

We heard a loud noise from the reception area, which was quickly followed by Junior Fisk rushing into the room. He had on a pair of old white and grey striped slacks, a purple undershirt, and bright green socks. He wasn't wearing shoes.

"I feel like I just got reamed by a proctological's middle finger," he said to the room at large. "Some fed woke me up, wantin' to know my life story in three words or less. Yes this, no that, 'til it wanted to drive me crazy. So I let it. I told that man I was a gun totin' Bible thumpin' red-necked bigot and if he remained one second longer in my home I'd shoot him dead. I don't know why the hell they're so damned worried about a corpse that very nearly killed me!"

"Junior," I said soothingly, "Sit down."

"I am an agitated man," he said, glancing wildly at Tally. "Why're you here?" he demanded of his friend.

"I had a visitor, too," Tallahassee said. "It ain't nothin' to rile yourself about, Junior. Cash and Stella are gonna take care of it."

Truer words were never spoken. We heard the doorbell ring.

"Here we go," Stella said to me. "You want, just nod whenever I look at you."

"I'm not without a voice," I said to her and smiled. "You two men repair to the restroom and be quiet," I said to Tally and Junior. "And I do mean quiet. These people eat conspiracy theories for breakfast."

When Stella opened the door, she was face to face with the man who had come to our defense two days ago outside the morgue.

"Well, well," he said to her. "Did you ever locate your missing fisherman cousin?"

"You got me there," she said dismissively. "Come on in. This whole thing is easy enough to explain."

As he walked into the front room, he looked at me. "Hello again," he said. "You'll remember me from Saturday. I'm Agent Clarkson. So, ladies, please explain. Why the story about your cousin?"

"We did not want to be involved with whatever is goin' on," Stella said. "Our only part in this is simple. A corpse came churnin' up from the depths of the ocean and blew a friend of ours out of his inner tube, displacin' him and presentin' us with something that had to be dealt with. So we dealt with it."

"Do you speak," he said to me. I thought I noticed a glint in his eyes. I wouldn't have bet on it, however.

"Often," I said to him. "Especially when I feel compelled by necessity. At the moment, I feel no such compulsion. What Stella has just told you is what there is to say about the incident."

"But just how do partygoers on a boat deal so effectively with such a unique situation?" he asked. "You didn't even radio the Coast Guard."

"Her father," I said to the man, "is the Sheriff of Brunswick

County." I didn't think I was telling Agent Clarkson anything he didn't already know. He was just following his orders and tying up loose ends.

"Yes," he said. "That jibes with what the Sheriff finally told us yesterday. I presume I don't have to tell you ladies that this is officially a matter of national security and to please remove it from your topics of conversation; but if I do, then here it is: Your government officially proscribes you from sharing any information with anyone regarding your recovery of a corpse from the Atlantic Ocean one mile offshore Southport, North Carolina last Saturday. This situation is sensitive and as serious as a heart attack. Are we clear?"

"Very," I said.

"Completely," Stella said.

"Fine," Agent Clarkson said. Then he smiled. "Thank you for your time. I wish it could have been under more congenial circumstances."

"Well," I said to him and moved rather quickly to walk him to the door, "we live in interesting times."

When he was gone, I looked at Stella. "They'll be hanging around for a while just to make sure we mind our Ps and Qs. But we need to drive to Bolivia. I want to know what Billy knows. I've always been a captive of my restless imagination. And when you get right down to it, I'm fundamentally opposed to being proscribed to do anything, especially by the federal government."

"It's gonna be nothin' but trouble, Cash," she said to me.

"When isn't it," I said.

"Well," Stella Conroy said with a note of resignation in her voice, "once in a blue moon, I reckon. And this, for certain, is not one of those times."

"That's the one showed up at my house," Tally said. "It surely sounds like somethin' important's goin' down."

Junior Fisk snorted and dropped into the swivel chair behind the desk we use for a reception area. I wondered if he could get out of it on his own steam. It fit him the way an unlined leather driving glove fits my hand: very tight. "Feds'll assign importance to most anything that strikes their fancy," he said. "Their main business is makin' mountains from anthills. Fools, all of them. You gonna take a look?"

"Hard to say," Stella said. She was walking back to the inner sanctum where we did most of our work. When she walked back a couple of minutes later, she had her Beretta in her right hand. "Y'all carrying?" she said to me.

"It's in the Jaguar's glove compartment," I said.

"Good. Let's mosey on over to Bolivia. See what daddy's got to say for himself."

"Well Junior," Tally said with a grin on his face, "are they gonna take a look? I vote yes."

I smiled. "Well, when you're right, you're right."

"Y'all be careful," Junior hollered at our backs as we walked out the door. Neither one of us bothered to answer him.

CHAPTER FIVE

Paul Sargasso was standing on a small slope where fifteen of his tillable acres were home to the next grapevines mature enough for harvesting. It was a beautifully manicured piece of land and the order it imposed on the rich brown dirt pleased him deep in his bones. His vineyard manager was up ahead doing what was now a daily inspection to determine the sugar content of the muscats that row after row would provide potable bottles of both grape juice and wine. Sargasso was both pleased and excited by the prospect of the coming harvest. There were ten more acres already in production, so this year his vineyard's yield would more than double, maybe even triple. Muscatel wine and grape juice was very popular here in North Carolina; its popularity reminded Sargasso of the Concord grape's success in New York State. People liked sugar.

In the far distance, he caught a glimpse of a sports car speeding alongside the five acres of strawberries and blueberries he also grew. Sargasso smiled. His younger brother Anthony was behind the wheel and he was forever in a hurry. Paul had always been close to his brother, despite their age difference. He was ten years older than Anthony, but their father had died when Paul was thirteen and Anthony was three. So Paul had been a surrogate father in those days for his younger brother and it had established what was to become the closest bond of Paul Sargasso's life. And now that they were both adults, they were creating a family legacy: Sargasso Enterprises.

Anthony was a chemist. His first job after graduating from Columbia University had been with DuPont, where he worked alongside a rather famous chemist intent upon creating a material that could withstand extreme assaults. It was an attempt to make body armor unnecessary. Although these efforts ultimately were unsuccessful, they did lead to several breakthroughs in related areas, and Anthony had found himself highly touted among his bosses at DuPont. But he was restless, and when his brother Paul had beckoned him with more interesting possibilities, he went without hesitation. Now he was chief winemaker at Sargasso Vineyards. He was also mixing, packaging, and distributing several designer drugs targeting the younger crowd. None was illegal. All were potent. Each was highly profitable.

Paul Sargasso did not care to know anything about the drug mixtures his brother developed and sold. He didn't care about designer drugs at all. But he did care about his enterprise's bottom line, and these strange concoctions of Anthony's were bringing in a small fortune. Last quarter, to his complete surprise, two drugs with chemical names he could not remember earned over four hundred thousand dollars after expenses. Anthony called them "Sweet Oats" and "April Rain" and he bagged them together under the acronym SOAR. Demand was extremely high and Anthony was having difficulty meeting it. In the very near future, he'd be hiring an assistant.

"Good sugar in the fourth and fifth and sixth rows, boss," his vineyard manager said, jarring Paul out of his reverie. "Rest is adequate for juice, better for wine. It's gonna be dandy, we get these grapes to storage. I'll meet y'all back at the main barn. A bunch of guys are waitin' on work. Time to hire? Whaddya think."

"Yes," Paul said. "Sign everybody who's here. We'll start in two weeks. If that's problematic for anyone, let me know. We don't want to lose them."

"That ain't a worry, boss. You're the man. They love you. If we had one, y'all'd be mayor around here. What's the pay? Same as last year?"

Paul Sargasso paused before he nodded. Then he said, "No. Up it to ten an hour this year. Impress upon them that their continued good work will result in wages continuing to rise. And say it with a smile, Moody."

"You don't gotta worry 'bout that none, boss," Moody Rawlins said. "I was born smilin'."

"I feel like I'm being watched," Jefferson Davis said to Cooper Grey.

The two men were wearing old jeans and work shirts and each had on a pair of high hip waders. They were standing in the middle of an inlet outside of Supply, North Carolina, checking on the saline content of the current coming and going into the ocean cutaway. They had thousands of baby oysters growing on this inlet floor and they were a few weeks away from their first harvest.

"It's what they do," Coop said. "They tire after a week or two of nothing."

"So you think I'm right? Not paranoid?" Jeff said to his friend and business partner.

"Look, Jefferson. I've never worked for the CIA but I have occasionally worked with them when I had a serious enough bond case that necessitated my going into Mexico or Canada. So do I think we're being watched because of that corpse? Maybe. Probably. The CIA is not in the business of trust. They disbelieve everybody. But we've done nothing to arouse their interest. If they're watching, they'll soon be gone."

"Still, I don't like it, Cooper. Big brother hasn't ever appealed to me. What's Stella thinkin'?"

Cooper Grey grinned a big face-cracking grin. "Hell, Jeff, what Stella's thinking and what Stella's saying are almost always two different things. I might venture to say the same of your girlfriend, Katherine Delaney. But do I think they're losing sleep over the worry of prying eyes? Hell no. They will do what they want to do and until a Mack truck stops them, that's just the way it is. Now lighten up. Let's test a few of these seedlings for taste and saline."

Both men felt a hit of excitement. They were now close to harvesting their first crop of oysters and so far their choice of this lagoon had proven to be ideal for the sweet taste and low salinity of the crop. If their luck held, they anticipated there'd be hundreds if not thousands of crates of oysters ready to be shipped to what was their growing list of buyers. And that list was expanding weekly to include grocery stores, specialty shops, fish markets, restaurants and food trucks.

An hour and a half later, the two men sat at the bar in Jack Mackerels, drinking dark Dos Equis and eating big fat shrimp with slices of lemon and horseradish sauce. It was one of their favorite places for lunch because the servings were substantial and the quality was always reliable.

"These shrimp local?" Coop said to the bartender, a guy named Roger whom he had known for years.

"You bet," Roger said. "Bought them this morning right off the pier up in Carolina Beach. Sweet, aren't they?"

"They are bodacious," Jeff Davis said, "and I could go for another helping. How about you, Coop?"

"You go ahead," Coop said. "I've got a hankering for a double cheeseburger with a side of onion rings. Two more drafts would be good, too, Roger."

The bartender nodded, pulled two big drafts of the dark brew, scribbled something on a piece of paper and walked back to the kitchen to place the order.

"See that guy in the far right booth behind us," Cooper Grey said to Jeff Davis when the bartender was out of earshot. "The one eating a burger and drinking coffee. Look in the mirror. Don't turn around."

"Uh huh," Davis said. "What about him?"

"He's most likely a fed," Coop said. "So yeah, I'd say we're being watched."

"He looks like a kid still in high school."

Cooper Grey smiled. "They grab them fresh out of the chute, Jefferson. That way, they can raise them to their satisfaction. He's probably thirty."

The cell phone that rang on the young man's table made him jump. He answered it, looked around the room, tossed a twenty dollar bill next to his plate and hurriedly left the restaurant.

"Well, something more important than us has just come up" Jeff Davis said.

"Let's hope it doesn't involve either one of our nosy, wayward women," Coop said. "Otherwise, he'll be back."

"It has something to do with the notion they know who may have killed Keats," Billy Conroy said to Stella and me. "Except they're sorta flummoxed, seein' as how the particular guy they have in mind is supposed to be dead himself."

"Say what?" Stella exclaimed.

"Y'all heard me," her father said.

"This does not sound good," I said, more to myself than to anyone else in the room. Louise was fixing cups of coffee and trying and failing to look uninterested.

Finally, I sucked in a big bunch of air, exhaled, and said, "So they think they may have a resurrection on their hands, one which they do not want to reach the light of day, and they're scrambling like crazy to contain the situation."

"Exactly right," the Sheriff said. "And they are as unhappy about this whole mess as a pig awaitin' slaughter."

"They're lookin' for someone in their ranks who may have turned?" Stella said.

"Yes," I said, taking a steaming mug of coffee from Louise.

"My friend at the Coast Guard Station in Oak Island told me they had a big hush-hush get-together with some civilian yesterday morning at their station in Wrightsville Beach," Louise Dickson said.

"Do you have a name," I asked her.

"All I know is Brooks. My friend didn't even know if that was a first name or a last name or even if it was a man or woman," said Louise, taking a seat in the chair next to Stella.

"Well, it ain't any of our concern," Billy Conroy said. "I really mean that and it is my final word on this precarious subject. But there is somethin' that is, and I could use your help with it," he said to Stella and me. "What do you two know about grapes?"

"They grow on vines," Stella said.

"And they're used to make juice, jelly, and wine," I added.

"Is there anything else, for Christ's sake," the Sheriff said, looking rather sternly at each of us.

"That depends, I suppose," I said to him. "Are you talking about a vineyard?"

"I am," he said.

"Well," I said, "they can be profitable after a while. But they take time to establish. I wouldn't exactly rank them among the top ten ways to try to amass a fortune quickly."

"What's this about, daddy," Stella said.

"It's about a man who owns a lot of land in Little Prong that is partially being put to use as a vineyard. He thinks his vines are being sabotaged by parties unknown. For all I know, he might could be correct but I can't see sending any of my men over there to poke around. They'd all be like bulls and china. I thought I'd deputize the two of you for a while and see what y'all could turn up. Might be nothin', might be somethin'. How 'bout it?"

"Little where?" I said.

"Little Prong," Stella said. "It's a bump in the road north west of here. It's sort of a gathering."

"That ain't the point, girls," Billy said. "Can you snoop around undetected long enough to see has this guy got a reason for his concern?"

"Well," I said and looked at Stella, "we can write an article."

"Exactly right," Stella said and grinned. "I snap photos, Cash takes notes, this guy whoever he is loves it, and maybe we find out what the hell he's so concerned about. How's that sound, daddy?"

"Fine and dandy," Sheriff Billy Conroy said. "Louise, go get the language. I need to deputize these two reprobates."

Five minutes later, Stella and I were upstanding members of North Carolina law enforcement. I have to admit, I really did not know whether or not I was happy about that.

CHAPTER SIX

Darius Millar, Attorney Mickey Huntley's multi-talented African American and handsome office manager, was at his desk in the reception area he occupied at the law office, drinking a glass of chilled sweet tea. It was twelve thirty in the afternoon and he had already had an exhausting morning, because his boss had been on a rampage over ongoing voting restrictions in North Carolina, and had therefore agreed to file an amicus brief supporting a case being brought by the local office of the ACLU to overturn the current legislation that infringed on those most basic rights.

Actually, when he really thought about it, she'd been on a rampage ever since the Democrats lost the state-wide election of 2012. And Sister Mary Louise, did they lose it. Everywhere you looked, you saw a big red ugly curb. You couldn't walk a block in Raleigh without tripping over some regressive Republican legislator or other. More than once, he'd heard his boss declare that the mission of the GOP was to return North Carolina to the Nineteen Fifties. Lately, she'd been declaiming that their bumper sticker for 2018 would simply be "Mission Accomplished." Unfortunately, she had a damn near perfect point.

As he stood up and started to walk over to the small kitchen attached to the office suite, a short, well-built woman with curly brown hair and light brown eyes, wearing a dark red pants suit and a pair of brown leather sandals without socks, entered the office foyer and looked around. Darius hurriedly put his glass in one of his desk drawers and went to meet her.

"May I help y'all?" he said to the woman.

It startled her for a moment. She'd had her back to him. Finally, she turned and said simply, "I don't really know."

Darius Millar smiled and said, "Well, there's lots of folks who feel that way at first. Let's go on into my office right through this archway and talk about whatever's on your mind."

"Are you Attorney Michael Huntley," the woman asked pleasantly.

"No ma'am," he said. "I'm her assistant. Mickey'll be back in a few minutes. She went to lunch."

"Michael Huntley is a woman?" she said skeptically.

"Yes ma'am. But it's not surprising you're confused. It's a long story, has to do with her mama naming her after a woman married one of those Barrymore actors. Why don't y'all take a seat right here. Would you like a glass of iced tea?"

"Well, I…" the woman started. Just at that moment, Mickey Huntley breezed through the front door with a look on her face that could have withered a bunch of freshly picked daisies.

"Darius," she said heatedly, "get that idiot Byron Jessup who calls himself a prosecutor on the phone. The frivolous asshole is still intent on filing charges in that ridiculous harassment complaint."

Darius Millar looked and her and cleared his throat rather loudly which had the usual effect on Mickey Huntley: she stopped in her tracks, focused on the room, and saw the woman sitting in the chair in front of her assistant's desk.

"This lady would like to speak with you about something as yet unspecified, boss," he said. "You've got a half hour before your next appointment. I expect that'll be enough time, won't it ma'am?" he said to the woman.

"If that's fine with you, it's fine with me," Mickey Huntley said. Her voice was completely devoid of the anger that had recently pervaded it. "I'm Mickey Huntley," she said to the woman and reached to shake her hand. "And you are…"

"Brooke Malanga," the woman said and stood to take the lawyer's outstretched hand. "I'm here to discuss the possibility of locating my brother, quietly, without attracting any outside attention."

"I don't really handle missing person cases," the lawyer said.

"But you must have access to people who do," the woman said. "Private investigators you trust and use. Your reputation precedes you, Attorney Huntley. And for what I have in mind I have to be able to rely on that reputation and whatever recommendations you may choose to share with me. Discretion, in this case, is not only the better part of valor; it is essential."

"I see," Mickey Huntley said. "In that case, perhaps I can assist you. Let's go into my office and talk about this further. Darius, please hold my calls for twenty minutes."

An hour and a half after leaving Carolina Beach, Stella and I drove to a four corners, where she said we'd arrived at our destination: Little Prong. We were sitting in the tan leather seats of my 1965 racing green Jaguar XKL that I'd recently had Buddy ship from Ithaca, New York to what was now my home in North Carolina. It had cost me a fortune and I could not have cared less. I loved her. But when I looked around at the landscape surrounding the car, there was nothing to see other than open fields, scrub brush, a few bunches of skinny oak trees, and a lot of blue sky.

"How can you tell," I said. "It's nothing but a four-way stop."

"Welcome to Little Prong," she said and grinned at me. "Turn left here on Little Prong Road. This guy Sargasso's vineyard is a few miles down."

Five minutes later, I slowed the Jag to a crawl. On the right side of the road was a large elevated sign that read "Sargasso Enterprises." On the left, an equally large and lighted sign that advertised "Muscatel Wines, Muscatel Juices from Sargasso Vineyards. Visitors Are Welcome."

"Huh," Stella said. "Looks like this guy Sargasso's got it goin' on. Let's mosey on up the vineyard road, see who we run into. At the very least, we're welcome."

The way in proved to be rather long and picturesque. We passed a turn of the century graveyard where more gravestones had fallen to the ground instead of standing upright on it, an old dilapidated homestead that had once been grand and impressive, several small copses of fir trees and scrub oak, until finally I saw an immense white pine barn with a red tin roof on the site where the paved road ended.

"This guy has no need to make money," I said to Stella. "He's already made it. That barn alone must have cost a couple of hundred thousand dollars. And that's not counting whatever it comes equipped with."

There was a designated parking area on either side of the road, so I pulled the Jag right, edged her up against the split rail bumper, and parked. As we got out of the car, a tall and hefty man with an incredibly deep tan, wearing overalls without a shirt and a pair of sneakers, approached us with a smile on his face.

"How y'all doin'?" he said.

"Good, good," Stella said. "Hell of a nice place you got here."

"Ain't it though," he said proudly. "Somethin' I can help you with? Our tours don't start 'til next month."

I smiled at him. "We're not here for a tour," I said. "We're freelancers. We spot things of interest around this area, write a story, take photographs, then we shop it to area publications in time for the summer season. Someone told us about the fine products you're creating here at the vineyard so we thought we'd see if you were amenable to letting us do an article on it."

"Wow," the guy said. "Boss'd love that. He's crazy for free publicity. Oh," he said. "It is free, ain't it?"

"As a bird," Stella said.

"Well," he said, "come on then. Boss's in the barn sipping from a couple barrels of his private stuff. Muscatel wine don't age. But we've got a few acres of cabernet we grow for wine and they sure as hell do. I'm Moody, by the way."

"I'm sorry?" I said. "You're what?"

"My name," he said and gave me a huge grin. "I'm Moody Rawlins. I manage these vineyards for Boss."

Beatrice Bush was sitting at a small, elegant table in her suite at the Hilton Wilmington Riverside Hotel drinking an intensely dry Bombay Gibson with five tiny pearl onions, which was accompanied by a double serving of Ruth's Chris Steak House's deservedly famous oysters Rockefeller. She was contemplating the potential disaster ahead of her and trying to determine just how badly her career would be damaged if she failed to accomplish what the Agency had asked of her—namely, find and neutralize a rogue agent named Eric Malanga, whom the Agency had already written off as just so much collateral damage.

I'd be finished, she finally told herself. Over, finis, kaput—say it as many ways as you like, it still amounts to the same thing. It was a ridiculous assignment when you came right down to it. This neophyte, this romantic gesture of a man the Agency had spent a fortune to train and educate, had somehow escaped a death sentence in a prison in, of all places, Myanmar, something no one had thought possible. And now he was back, collecting on the outstanding debts of those he believed had betrayed him. But where the hell was he? She had no clue. And in this section of this goddamn fucking state where everything looked like something out of Mayberry once you left Wilmington, she'd need a veritable army of scouts to help her track down this idiot before he could conclude what he'd started with Woody Keats.

The sister had been less than useless. She knew nothing about everything when it came to her brother. They hadn't been close as children growing up because she'd been nearly six years older than Eric. She thought she remembered he'd liked taking things apart and putting them back together again. Well, duh! Now it seemed his preference rested with the taking-things-apart half of that equation. And, she said, he'd had a lovely soprano singing voice. Big whoop! Now, if there was anything remotely musical about him, it was as useful to her as a fireman in Hades.

Beatrice Bush sighed deeply and loudly before picking up her phone to call Bart Clarkson. He answered on the first ring.

"Clarkson," he said. "What's up, Bea?"

"Where's your twin," she said.

"Keeping an eye on the sister," he said.

"Anything interesting?"

"Not really," he said. "She went to see somebody in a building on

Front Street this afternoon. It's a four-story building with about two hundred offices in it. Because she's in concierge banking, he guessed she was visiting a client. Why?"

"Call him off. She doesn't know a thing that we need. And those people who bumped into the body are also useless for our purposes. Call all of the surveillance off and then come see me."

"Alone?"

"Of course alone," she said. "I don't need company for what I have in mind for you, big boy."

"See you in ten," he said hurriedly.

As she finished the Gibson and enjoyed the last of the oysters Rockefeller, Beatrice Bush decided that she might as well accept the perks of her job for as long as possible. I could be wandering around in the wilderness for years if this job goes haywire. Little did she know how right she was, both literally and figuratively.

CHAPTER SEVEN

Cassandra Quick watched the long, low, dark green car glide along the road toward the vineyard barn and wondered who was inside and why they were visiting. It was an idle thought. She'd been sitting in what was left of the front parlor of the old homestead on Sargasso land for the better part of the day, practicing deep breathing in order to increase her store of patience—something she often did. She needed nightfall before she could begin the next phase of her impulsion to disrupt the life of Paul Sargasso.

She had told her cousin Cuddy that she planned to destroy more newly planted vines and then intentionally leave a trail of footprints that went, eventually, nowhere. This is what she was reconsidering: where to have the footprints lead Sargasso or one of his minions. After a while, she smiled. I'll let those footprints coax him from those vines, down the berm where his cabernets are planted, across the dirt road running next to the main artery, and disappear them right beside the old gravestone of my great-great-grandmother. Just as she'd finished this new consideration of her plan, the same long, low, dark green car again passed by, leaving the vineyard the same way it had entered. It was now time to nap, she knew. The sun was much lower in the sky than when that car had arrived. Cassandra closed her eyes, softly intoned the Little People of her family's folklore legend, sighed, and went deeply to sleep.

———————————————————

It was happy hour by the time Stella and I returned to the cottage on Beach House Lane. Jeff and Coop had the grill going while Sarah and Mickey were fixing drinks at a table they'd set up in the middle of the patio. Across the ocean and infusing this tableau with light was a cacophony of color on the horizon, a wild mélange of orange, purple, and gold as the sun prepared to set for the day.

"Hey, girls, how'd it go," Coop said.

"It went," Stella said noncommittally as she eyed the pitcher of vodka Collinses that Sarah was stirring. "I am going to want a martini right about now," she said to nobody in particular. "Cash?"

"Make it two," I said. "What's cooking, fellas?"

"Oysters from our very own crop," Jefferson Davis said proudly. "We found a couple three dozen big enough to take, so we did. Po-boys on the way, ladies."

"Cash," Mickey Huntley said, "will you join me inside for a minute? Something's come up that probably requires your and Stella's attention."

"Sure."

Stella was in the kitchen pouring Grey Goose into two rocks glasses filled with ice and three olives each. She looked over her shoulder at us.

"What's goin' on?" she said.

"Something Sarah says you two wouldn't touch with a thousand-foot pole," Mickey Huntley said.

"What might that be?" I said.

"A woman came to see me today," Mickey said. As Stella handed me my drink, I took a sip, smiled with satisfaction, and waited for the lawyer to continue. "Anyway," Mickey said, "she needs help locating her brother. Wants discretion, doesn't want to raise alarms, can afford whatever it takes, things like that."

"I don't right off see a problem with this, Mick," said Stella. "Is there one I can't see?"

"Yes," Mickey said. "Her name is Brooke Malanga. Name ring any bells?"

"Nope," said my partner.

"Good god," I said loudly, nearly at the same time. Stella stared at me. "Remember what Louise told us? The CIA had a meeting with somebody named Brooks."

"Exactly," said Mickey Huntley.

Stella stood there silently for a minute or so, drained her nearly full glass of vodka, coughed, and muttered, "Well shut the fuckin' front door. There can't be but two people alive who'd believe in such coincidence. I surely don't and yet it happened. I need a cigarette. I need another drink."

"You need to realize I had no idea of your connection to this thing before Sarah finally enlightened me," Mickey Huntley said. "Otherwise, I would never have recommended you to Ms. Malanga. But Sarah is nothing if not discreet, especially when it comes to you two and your business. So I did recommend you. And she's on her way here to meet with you both."

"What? When?" I said.

"Couple of hours," she said. "Unless I call her and cancel."

"You do realize the CIA could still have eyes on us," I said. The lawyer nodded. "Stella?" I said. She was back in the kitchen, pouring more vodka into her glass. "Cancel?"

"It'll be dark in a couple hours," Stella said.

"Sure," I said, "but then the sun inevitably comes up again. What's your point?"

"Your point, actually," my partner said. "Y'all don't cotton to bein' proscribed from doin' anything, especially by the big bad government."

Those words could not have hit me any harder than if she'd slugged me right across my stubborn jaw. I felt giddy and stunned at the same time. Words to eat by and they were mine.

"I was aware of being followed," Brooke Malanga said to Stella and me. We were sitting in our private back office on Lake Park Boulevard. "When I saw him turn away as I was driving home, I realized he'd been pulled off. I can't imagine why, if they've given up watching me, they would still persist in watching you. After all, you did nothing except discover by accident a corpse."

"I'm sure you're right," I said to her. "Why don't you tell us what's on your mind and how we may be able to help?"

"It's difficult to explain," she said.

"We're real good at interpretin' inferences," Stella said. "Just go ahead and start."

"Well," the woman said, "a few days ago I got a postcard in the mail. But it's not really about that. But that's important. It's, oh, it's that my brother and I aren't really close but we love each other and I want to try to find him."

I realized that she was trying to frame a story for us that she very nearly couldn't understand herself.

"Who is your brother?" I asked.

That seemed to focus her. "Eric," she said. "Eric Malanga."

"And why is the CIA interested in him?" Brooke Malanga nodded, as though she understood why I was asking these questions. She probably did.

"When he was twenty one, just out of Princeton, they recruited him," she said.

"And he's how old now?" Stella said.

"Thirty three. He'll be thirty four in August." Brooke Malanga stood up from the chair she'd chosen to sit in and began to walk around the office. Finally, she said, "My brother is a genius, really. He's a poet and a gifted mathematician; even though those two fields seem entirely unrelated, they're not. He's also a natural linguist and mimic. He speaks a dozen languages, including various iterations of Chinese. I believe it was his language skills that first drew the attention of the CIA."

"Because..." Stella said.

"The Agency wanted more of a clandestine presence on the Pacific Rim," she said. "Once they'd trained and educated him to their satisfaction, they sent him to Indonesia to run a program that offered English as a second language to select students of targeted Indonesians they had an interest in."

"And your brother knew this?" I asked.

"That's the problem," she said. "I don't believe he did entirely. What I have just said is my opinion only. He told me he was going to Indonesia under a program sponsored by the CIA to develop English language skills for potential graduate students in engineering. At the time, I have to admit I was skeptical. But he was thrilled. He believed he'd be making a difference in the world and that fit his idealism perfectly."

"And then something went wrong," my partner said.

"Apparently, yes. But I can only speculate," Brooke said.

"Please do," I said.

"I used to get postcards from Eric over the years. They were always positive and upbeat. A few years ago, he met an Indonesian woman he fell in love with and wanted to marry. He said he and she planned to come to the United States; he was going to quit his job and move on to a new phase of his life. Then I heard nothing more from him and after several years had passed, I was forced to presume he was dead because my inquiries to the CIA fell on deaf and dumb ears; that is, until a few days ago when I got a postcard with a picture of wildflowers and a two-word message, 'Remember Ivanhoe.' I have no idea what the message means. But I thought it could be from Eric."

"And then the CIA asked to meet with you." Stella said.

She looked at Stella and nodded. "And I knew. He's alive. And I presume they believe he murdered that man you found floating in the ocean. Apparently, from what little they shared with me, the man recruited Eric. I don't know whether or not he did kill Mr. Keats. But if he did, he must have had a very good reason.

My brother is not a sociopath. But I also believe they want to locate and kill him, although they never uttered the word kill. They always say something like terminate his employment. I'd like to find him first. I want to prevent that. So," Brooke Malanga said quietly to Stella and me, "Will you help me?"

I looked at Stella. She was fiddling with a pencil and her left foot was tapping softly against the carpeted floor. Eventually, she looked over at me and smiled. All she said was, "Nicky Sorge."

Our visitor had no idea what those two words meant. I did. Nicky Sorge was a man I had chosen to terminate for a very good reason. And Stella had chosen to help me.

"How can we not," I finally said. Brooke Malanga breathed a sigh of relief. I hoped I was the only one in the room who heard the reluctance that animated my voice.

CHAPTER EIGHT

"We'll be needing somethin' reliable to drive," Tallahassee Bodine said to Stella and me. "Junior's Ford takes a notion to drop dead just about any time of the day or night. I ain't wanna be stuck in rural Brunswick County at two o'clock in the mornin'. I am not suicidal."

"We'll rent a car, Tally," I said. "I don't think it'll take the two of you very long to figure out if anything unusual is going on at Sargasso's vineyard."

"Y'all just be real clear you're lookin' for work," Stella said to him. "He told us the other day he needs more pickers. And we've got to spend some time on a new case needs our attention."

"Junior ain't exactly pickin' material, Stella," Tally said. "I'll admit he's close to the ground. Trouble is, he don't bend too easy."

"The guy who manages the place is Moody Rawlins," I said. "He needs drivers for the trucks they use to haul the grapes from the vineyards. And Junior could also sort the stems from the fruit. You two can definitely handle Moody. He'll be your new best friend in less than five minutes flat."

Out of the blue, Stella said to him, "If I told you to remember Ivanhoe, Tally, what would y'all say?"

"Say what?" he said. "Remember what?"

"Ivanhoe," she said. "It means something but we don't know exactly what."

"I got no earthly idea, Stella," Tally said. "It don't mean nothin' to me."

Just as he'd spoken, Junior Fisk walked into the office. "Remember Ivanhoe?" Tally said to him.

"Hell yes. I most assuredly do," Junior said. "The last time I drove through there I got a speeding ticket. Cost me three hundred bucks. They piggybacked court costs on top of the fine. I was only doin' forty in a thirty-mile zone. I hate that place."

I looked at Stella. She was shaking her head from side to side and grinning. Thanks to Junior Fisk, we may have just discovered the starting point for our search for Eric Malanga. I am always amazed by serendipity.

Cassandra Quick and her cousin Cudworth Sweat were sitting beside the gravesite of Cuddy's grandfather's brother in the little cemetery situated on Paul Sargasso's land, eating a picnic lunch of cornbread biscuits and cold cucumber soup. It wasn't an unusual occurrence: folks often visited the designated site to spend time with those who had passed. It was early afternoon and there was a cool breeze that mitigated the heat of the day. The cemetery was over 150 years old, and it had been consecrated Lumbee land when it was established. There were generations of Lumbee buried here and a good many were ancestors of Cassandra and her cousin Cuddy. They had been sitting there since dawn and they both looked up when they heard voices coming toward them.

"Here he comes," Cassandra said.

"He's not alone," Cuddy said.

"He's a man doesn't like to be alone," she said. "Put your sunglasses on. We don't want him lookin' us in the eye."

"Won't be close enough for that," Cuddy said. "Two hundred feet away at least."

"He'll wander once he sees us," Cassandra said to him.

Paul Sargasso and his vineyard manager Moody Rawlins were walking across the small cemetery when they suddenly stopped. "What the hell?" Sargasso said. "What in the god damned hell?"

"Please don't cuss in a graveyard, boss," Moody Rawlins said. "It's terrible bad luck to agitate the spirits."

"Spirits," Sargasso said loudly. "What the fuck does this have to do with spirits? I've got a vandal running loose on my property for Christ sake, Moody. Two more rows of grapevines destroyed. And this. A trail of footprints leading here, to this old dump. Where is that idiot who calls himself a Sheriff?"

Moody Rawlins, although he was not a Catholic, closed his eyes and crossed himself. When he opened them, he saw Cassandra and Cuddy watching the scene. "Boss," he said quietly, "people yonder visiting a grave. Might could be they saw somethin'."

Paul Sargasso considered this, composed himself, and decided to walk over and talk with the visitors. "Good day," he said to them. "Have you been here long?"

"Maybe an hour," said Cassandra Quick. "We like to visit Samuel on his birthday. Why? Are we trepassin' or something?"

"Oh no. No, no; nothing like that. I was just wondering if you'd perhaps seen anyone else while you've been paying your respects."

"Not a soul," Cuddy said. "It's always peaceful. We enjoy the peace."

"You're welcome anytime," Sargasso said. "But if you ever should see someone who seems suspicious or out of place, could you alert my manager over there?"

"We could," Cassandra Quick said.

Sargasso smiled at them, tipped his head in thanks, and turned to walk away. Once he and Moody Rawlins were out of earshot, Cudworth Sweat said to Cassandra Quick, "We could, Mr. Sargasso. But you'd best believe we won't."

———————————————————————

The Black River runs for fifty miles through three counties in North Carolina and eventually joins the Cape Fear River ten miles above Wilmington, where it eventually flows to the sea. One of the three counties it travels through is Sampson, where it borders the small community of Ivanhoe, a Census Designated Place. The river is one of the cleanest, high quality waterways in the state and is home to plentiful fish and mussels. Eric Malanga thought about how much he loved this river and how it had sustained him as he kayaked from his small shelter in an overgrown and unused plot of frontage on the outskirts of Ivanhoe to where he was going to fish for his dinner that day. As he paddled, he heard the melody of songbirds following along his path. He had finally identified two of these musicians: the yellow throated vireo and the prothonotary warbler.

He was a tall, well-muscled man who now passed easily as mixed race because he spent entire days in the sun and his skin was so deep a brown only his finely drawn features hinted at his Caucasian heritage. He was hoping to net some smallmouth bass, but he'd be happy with whatever hit his hook: catfish or paddlefish or even a largemouth bass. He'd stocked up on a passel of wild blueberries an hour ago, and his tomatoes and potatoes and lettuces were all abundant and ready for his evening meal. He felt rich.

Then, as it always did, his mind drifted to his fiancé, Anjay. He felt himself being overtaken by a melancholy so profound, he knew he could die from this grief. His beloved Anjay, the woman he had honored, loved, and cherished was dead. He thought of her first words to him when she'd first entered his classroom in Bali. "My name is Anjay. It means unconquerable in your English. I need to learn better your English." Now, she lived only in his memory. He had been so happy. They had been deeply in love and shared many of the same interests: poetry, music, a passion for seeking what is spiritual in their lives. At first, when the trouble started, he hadn't recognized it for what it was. And by the time the full weight of what lay ahead for her hit him, it was too late. She was gone and he found himself in a Myanmar prison where he was expected to die. The guilt he now lived with was the injustice of her death, which was ultimately because of her relationship with him. There was nothing he could do to assuage it.

Eric Malanga suddenly realized he'd nearly drifted into shore, and back paddled to where he wanted to fish. A swarm of insects was hovering where he dropped his line. He was using minnows for bait. Fifteen minutes later, he'd hooked a two pound catfish and two smallmouth bass. He'd cook them all tonight. He was hungry and tomorrow he'd begin his second quest for the next man on his list: the master sergeant who had refused to forward his calls of distress, Clay Carpenter, who was stateside now, only a couple of hours from where Eric Malanga turned his kayak around and paddled back to his shelter in the woods by the side of the Black River, just outside of the small community of Ivanhoe.

Anthony Sargasso was finishing up his week's worth of work in the large barn across the road from the vineyards. He was weighing and packaging the weekly supply of his two wildly popular designer drugs. He had a very successful model for distribution: his street buyers sold to their own customers. Anthony had no part in that distribution. He was strictly wholesale. What his suppliers did after they'd purchased that week's supply didn't concern him at all. He let them charge what their particular piece of the market would bear. His charge was simple: each packet he sold cost that street distributor twenty dollars a packet. He never asked what the charge was ultimately to the buyer. He didn't care.

Currently, his list of suppliers totaled fifty people. He had another twenty or so on a waiting list, which he would begin to chip away at when he hired an additional chemist, something he expected to do within a week. His largest distributors came down from Raleigh. Two or three of them bought one hundred packets each week. It always amazed him. Last year, he had cleared $400,000. This year, he would clear $750,000. His brother Paul would be slack-jawed when Anthony gave him this news. This made the chemist smile. He liked to surprise and please his brother.

He heard the sound of footsteps behind him on the plank floor and turned to see one of his customers walking towards him. "You're right on time, as usual," he said to the young man. "Your order's ready."

"Can y'all spare six extra," the guy said. "I picked me up a couple more customers. Referrals. Your shit's the best on the street."

"Not this week," Anthony answered. "I'm tight. Next week, most likely. I'm hiring help. You wanna go down for six more next week?"

"Yes. For sure, then? I don't want to promise and get caught empty-handed."

"For sure," Sargasso said, making a note on his order sheet.

When Tallahassee Bodine and Junior Fisk walked up to the man sorting papers in the huge barn that held the various machines and vats that turned grapes into wine, Junior tapped him on the small of the back and then cleared his throat. The man, momentarily startled, turned to see who had poked him.

"Somethin' I can help y'all with," he said to the two of them, looking each of them over and being obvious about it. They were quite a sight. Junior had on a pair of overalls with a bright orange tee shirt underneath, and a pair of high-top white sneakers. Tally was sporting a pair of red plaid pants, a purple long-sleeved cotton dress shirt and a pair of spit-polished black loafers without socks. Both of them wore baseball caps that advertised The Fat Pelican Saloon.

"Might could be," Junior said, smiling at him. "I am Junior Fisk and this here's my friend

Tallahassee Bodine. We heard y'all was hiring."

"I am," Moody Rawlins said.

"That is fine," Tally said and extended his hand, which Rawlins reached for and shook.

"Cause we're lookin'."

"I need experienced hands, boys" Moody said.

"I have been picking since I was old enough to stand upright," Tally said proudly. "I am so fast and true I am unrivaled."

"He picks, I sort," Junior said. "I may be fat, but I'm swift."

Moody Rawlins looked away for a moment and decided that he liked these two men he had never seen around these parts before. "Where y'all from," he asked.

"Closer to the beach than here," said Junior. "But there ain't enough work to keep the cold out of our bones come winter. So we're movin' inland where we can hope to survive."

"Well, I need a serious picker for Mr. Sargasso's cabernets. He's the boss of this place and I got five acres about ready. I'm paying ten dollars an hour. If that interests y'all," he said to Tally, "consider yourself hired."

"Yessir, boss," Tally said and grinned. "I am a very interested man and that sounds sweet to me."

"Now you," Moody said, turning to Junior Fisk, "I can use you in the big barn separating stems from grapes. Pay's the same. Okay?"

"I'm grateful," Junior said.

"Y'all can start tomorrow. Be here at seven. We work a full ten-hour day with an hour for lunch and two fifteen-minute breaks."

At five fifteen the following afternoon, Tallahassee Bodine was standing at the side of the road next to the vineyards that held the cabernet grapes when Junior Fisk stopped to pick him up in the five-year-old rental car, an orange Kia, to drive home to Carolina Beach. He'd been in the vineyards all day, picking. Junior had been in the main barn, sorting grapes from stems.

"Somethin's goin' on in that big building 'cross the way," Tallahassee said. "I musta seen three, four dozen boys and girls comin' and goin' all day."

"Boys and girls?" Junior said.

"Eighteen, nineteen, y'all get my drift; nothin' in their hands goin' in; nothin' comin' out. And none of 'em was poor. Looked like money to me."

"Cocaine slips into a pocket easy enough," Junior said.

"But they wasn't tryin' to hide nothin', including themselves. I wanted, I couldda got a photo of any one of them."

"So you're suggesting nothin' illegal?"

"I guess I am," Tallahassee said.

"Well, we'll lay it out for the girls; let them figure out what they want to do next," Junior said.

"I'm kinda curious, Junior. If we eat a bite in Shallotte, relax a bit, we might could drive back here later and figure it out our own selves, save Stella and Cash some time, especially if it ain't related to the trouble the man thinks he has."

"Y'all are aware of the curious cat," said Junior Fisk.

"Uh huh," Tallahassee answered. "I am. But last time I looked, I ain't a cat."

CHAPTER NINE

The town that was Ivanhoe, North Carolina was a little over an hour's drive from our office on Lake Park Boulevard in Carolina Beach. We were in Stella's Mustang rather than my Jag, mainly because it was more comfortable and the roads weren't always good for delicately balanced classic automobiles.

We were heading into Wilmington to pick up Route 41 when I said to her. "How do I register to vote around here? Sarah's been on my case about it for the last six months and she won't stop until I do it."

"Well, that should not surprise you, Cash," Stella said. "Sarah is nothing if not political. Why the hell haven't y'all done it already? "

"I'm registered in New York," I said. "I voted absentee ballot last time. I always vote. And Sarah damned well knows it."

"Look here," Stella said to me, "Y'all live here now, not there, and North Carolina is not New York—not by a long and winding country mile. Hell, in 2008, when Obama beat whoever he was running against, he won this state and every bigot here went crazy as a shithouse rat. And they're still crazy. So this state needs your vote a lot more than New York does."

"Well," I said, "Okay. I'll register tomorrow."

Forty minutes later, I was beginning to think about a sandwich rather than politics when Stella said to me, "This is it," as we drove along what resembled a main street. "Welcome to Ivanhoe."

To say only that it was small might imply that a couple thousand people inhabited it. In fact, only around three hundred people did. And they were mostly either planting and picking blueberries or raising and slaughtering pigs. There were no stoplights, very few streets, one restaurant called Breath of Life that did not sound appetizing, a grocery store named Bettin' On Blue with a slogan that read "Pee Dabbers Do It Best," some sort of business that dealt in construction, and another that mined minerals. There was a post office and one doctor, in case somebody got sick. The majority of business establishments were farms. Every single one of the folks I saw walking or sitting or driving was black.

"Looks as though there's a dearth of Caucasians around here," I said. "How come?"

"They're around," said Stella. "A lot of good farm work attracts who lives here, mostly. Let's hit the post office. Maybe whoever sent that postcard to Brooke did it direct from here."

The little guy who ran the post office looked as old as Methuselah, but he was lively and he liked to talk. "How can I help you lovely ladies today," he said to Stella and me and took a little bow.

"We're fixin' to see if y'all recognize somebody we're hoping to visit with today," Stella said to him.

"Okie dokie," he said, as Stella handed him the shot she had of Eric Malanga. I watched him go from curious to indifferent in about three seconds flat. Then he looked back at the two of us and smiled.

"He is no one I have ever laid eyes on before," the man said; then he added, "not that I want to sound unhelpful, but I know every white man in Ivanhoe and I have never seen this fellow in my life. Is he wanted for something? Is there reason for concern, because if there is I am obligated to inform as many people as can to be on the lookout for him?"

"Not at all," I said to mollify the man. "A girl is looking for her brother, and she remembered that they used to summer here so she thought he might have returned."

"Oh, well then," the postmaster said. "I'm sorry I couldn't be of more help. But believe me, ladies. This man is not in Ivanhoe."

As we were walking out of the Post Office, and unbeknownst to us, Eric Malanga was crossing the town's main street a few hundred feet from where we stood.

CHAPTER TEN

Beatrice Bush was sitting in a reclining chair in her hotel room at the Wilmington Riverside Hilton at eight o'clock in the evening, staring at the ornate clock on the living room wall. She watched seconds hang a bit before they progressed. This is a metaphor for my life she thought, although she wasn't sure if it was a metaphor or a symbol. What the hell difference did it make what it was; it was her life and the hourglass wasn't on her side.

Earlier today, she had dispatched a couple hundred operatives, in pairs, to visit each and every post office in southeastern North Carolina and northeastern South Carolina, to see if anyone could attest to actually having recently seen Eric Malanga. So far, she'd heard back from a few dozen, all with negative reports. To say she was unhopeful would be an understatement. When her "private/private" line rang, she knew instantly who was calling.

"Yes, sir," she said when she picked up the phone.

"Anything?" asked her boss, Director for Internal Affairs Roland Bishop.

"Nothing but negatives," she said. "I've got a lot more operatives to hear from before I'll know. It'll take another few days."

"Did you decide to target post offices in South Carolina that run along the border?"

"Yes," she said. "I wouldn't put it past him to try to confuse us by hiding in Marlboro, Horry, or even Dillon County. I recruited some help from the State Police in Charlestown for that."

"For all we know, Malanga may be finished now that Keats is dead. We just don't know enough to make a decision one way or another. Officially, we can't even dispute that Medical Examiner's finding of cause of death." Bishop said. "It's going to read "undetermined.""

"Unofficially?" was all she said.

"Foul play. That gives us latitude to find for suicide as well as homicide," he said.

"And you?" she asked.

Roland Bishop sighed. "Let's face it, Bea," he said. "Either way the probable proximate cause was Malanga if it is Malanga. To me that's some kind of felony."

"Yes," Beatrice Bush said. "I issued an extremely dangerous/shoot-on-sight-if-necessary order through back channels." But Bishop had already hung up.

Cassandra Quick walked into the post office in Pembroke, North Carolina, where she had rented a mailbox for the past decade. She was in a hurry. Her cousin Cuddy had called her earlier that morning to tell her something was going on at the Sargasso Estate. He hadn't elaborated, but she was meeting up with him in two hours and she needed to hustle. As she inserted her key into the mailbox, she noticed two well-built men wearing pressed black suits with starched white shirts and bright blue ties, complemented by dark socks and spit-polished black cordovans. They were talking with the postmaster at the end of the lobby. She quieted her breathing and listened. This is what she heard.

"...and some urgency," said suit number one, handing the postmaster what looked like a photograph. She watched as the man studied it before he spoke.

"I don't think...but what's goin'...is this...dangerous?"

"Yes...very...do not approach...my card." suit number two said, taking a business card out of his jacket pocket. "Let him...and then...immediately."

"Day or night," suit number one said over his shoulder as the two were walking out.

Cassandra made a fast decision as she hurried over to the postmaster. "What the heck was that all about, Jimmy? Y'all looked so serious."

Jimmy Fish gave her a weak smile. "CIA's lookin' for a guy they say's a murderer."

Cassandra did what she always did when she wanted to know more: she let her face release all expression.

"That the guy?" she asked.

"Yeah and I ain't never seen him before in my life," said Jimmy Fish, handing her the photograph. The minute Cassandra glanced at the picture of a smiling young man in some sort of uniform, she felt her pulse quicken. But her face remained blank along with her voice.

"Me neither," she said, returning the photo to the postmaster as she flipped through her photographic memory to recall just when and where she had seen this man before. "Well, don't worry on it, Jimmy; he's likely not hanging around these parts," Cassandra said as she turned and walked out of the post office.

She was driving down route 76 East to Little Prong Baptist Church to rendezvous with her cousin when she remembered. A few months ago she'd been fishing for catfish on the Black River when she'd met another fisherman: the man she'd seen a photo of in the Pembroke post office. He'd been fishing downstream from her and slowly they'd drifted into each other's orbit. Although there were differences in his appearance—he was a deep-brown color now from the sun and his hair was nearly shoulder length and bleached lighter by the sun—his facial features were clearly identical.

"That man's no murderer," Cassandra said quietly to herself. He'd been pleasant and remarkably polite. However, there had also been a profound sadness about him, as though he'd been broken by something from which he would never heal. They'd spent fifteen minutes in companionable if subdued conversation that ranged from warblers to the myriad fish that called the Black River home. She recalled he had mentioned living beside the river. He had not indicated where. She also realized they'd never even exchanged names. But Cassandra was undaunted. What she did know was that she'd been in the neighborhood of Ivanhoe where several of her cousins lived. She'd find this man and warn him of what clearly looked to her like life-threatening danger. And if he asked for her help, she would give it. Cassandra had studied well on the Big Boss Man. She knew his wiles and his ways. And she was also a participant in the current and very active Underground Railroad whose current purpose, while different from its original one, was still to shelter innocent people from the long arm of the law.

"There is more dang powders and plants and mason jars and Bunsen burners than a witch's coven," Junior Fisk said to Stella and me. "But from what we could tell, none of whatever's goin' on there has got a thing to do with the one grows grapes, Paul Sargasso."

"Yeah," Tally said. "It's just the brother, by himself. And he keeps a big list with alls the people who buy from him—names, phone numbers, money paid. It just ain't possible what he's doing's illegal, Cash. Anybody snoopin' could find out all that's goin' on so quick you'd miss them even lookin' if y'all blinked."

Stella lit a cigarette and turned her swivel chair around to stare out the big back window in our suite of offices that overlooked the rear parking lot. Our garbage bins nearly filled it. "Whaddya thinking," she said to the window she was facing.

"It's probably designer drugs that the authorities haven't caught up with yet," I said. "Every once in a while we'd get one or two of them in Ithaca. They'd be real popular until some student overdosed and either died outright or thought he could tightrope walk across a bridge railing that spans one of our many gorges and fell a few hundred feet into one of them."

"Helluva gaff," Stella said.

"But if it ain't illegal, what's the beef with Mr. Sargasso all about?" Junior said to the room.

"Anthony Sargasso's likely sideways with a private citizen," Stella said. "And whoever it is has decided to include Paul Sargasso as well."

"Say what?" asked Tally.

"Some young kid is dead or badly hurt or missing because of ingesting this undetermined, mind-altering concoction," I said. "And revenge is on somebody's mind."

"Exactly right," Stella said as she opened her sideboard to grab a bottle of bourbon that Tally had brewed at the Sawtelle brothers' still. When she swiveled back around to face the three of us, she nodded to Junior. "Grab four glasses from the kitchenette, please, Mr. Fisk. We've all got some more thinking and planning to do."

"It was late," Cudworth Sweat said to Cassandra Quick. "Eleven thirty, thereabouts. I was on my way home from a meeting in Shallotte; there were no lights but you couldn't miss the flashlight beam. So I stopped and parked across the road and waited."

They were sitting comfortably on a bench at the side of the old Baptist Church on Route 76 in the populated place known as Little Prong. They were also very close to Sargasso's Estate and they could hear the soft hum of activity going on at the vineyard. The day was full of that intense bright sunshine that fairly defines summer along the Carolina coastal lands. Cuddy was perspiring; his cousin wasn't. Cassandra said nothing.

"About ten minutes in, I seen the two of them," Cuddy said. "A tall skinny black guy wearing a pair of honest-to-god lime green pants that seemed to glow in the dark and a short, fat, white dude wearing blue overalls. I had to chuckle they looked so odd. They didn't rush. They just ambled a ways down the highway away from me and then 'bout five minutes later they come driving past me on their way back towards the coast."

Still, Cassandra said nothing. "So early this morning I drove over to the vineyard and set awhile in the graveyard waiting for the sun to rise." Cuddy said. ""Bout quarter 'til seven here the two of them come again. The white dude's driving and he lets the black guy off in front of those wine grapes that are nearly across the road from where I'm at. Then he drives up and parks in the lot and walks up to the barn and disappears. So they're both working at the vineyard."

The two cousins sat in silence for a long two minutes. Finally, Cassandra said, "What car are they driving?"

"Older Kia." said Cuddy. "Orange. The fat one drives. You gonna take it?"

"Yes," she said. "I'll follow them home. We need to know are they undercover cops or working for a rival or just what is going on."

"Well, we may not know what, exactly," said Cuddy. "But it's for certain there is something going on."

"We'll know what it is by this time tomorrow," said Cassandra Quick.

CHAPTER ELEVEN

Cooper Grey was humming one of his favorite songs, an old classic that the late great Rosemary Clooney sang to perfection, entitled "Do You Miss New York?" He was also cleaning out one of the engine compartments on the Portofino because sometime in the recent past some oil had spilled from a half empty can and the entire hold was a stupefying mess. He was also wondering where the hell Tallahassee Bodine was. This was due to the fact that Tally was supposed to be right here, helping Coop with the cleanup. So he wiped off his hands, grabbed his cell phone and voice-dialed a number he had long since memorized.

After five rings, a robotic voice told him he could leave his message after the beep. Cooper swore a bit under his breath, hung up without leaving any message, and pocketed his cell phone. As Jeff Davis walked up from the galley carrying a couple of Dos Equis Dark, Coop said,

"Where's Tally hanging these days? He's not back in Myrtle Beach playing poker, is he?"

"No idea," Jeff said. "Why?"

"Cause I asked him a few days ago to help me with this cleanup.

He said he would. But I've called him three times and he doesn't answer his phone. You think we ought to check on him? He might be sick; incapacitated, even."

"If he was sick, first thing he'd do is call Junior and Junior would call Stella and so on and so forth," Jeff said.

"Still," said Coop, trying to get at a little puddle of oil that required a tiny mitt to reach it.

Jefferson Davis took a huge swig of beer, belched, looked out at the deep blue of the Atlantic Ocean, thought about having dinner and then sex with Cash Delaney and finally said, "I'll scoot on over there when I finish this Dos Equis. It won't take me more than ten minutes."

"Good deal," Coop said.

When Jefferson Davis used his key and walked into the Sawtelle brothers' house where Tallahassee Bodine now lived, the only thing he heard was nothing. He glanced around and saw that everything was in order. The kitchen, with its narrow refrigerator, double sink, potbelly stove, and big upright freezer was neat as a pin. The old polished rolltop desk where Tally kept track of the comings and goings of visitors to the site was orderly, as usual. And both big, comfortable chairs that fronted the massive stone fireplace were exactly where they always were.

Nothing was out of place and nothing suggested any sort of trouble. He rummaged through a bunch of old Island Gazettes and an assortment of bills until he saw a hand drawn map and a note composed in what he instantly recognized as Cash Delaney's handwriting. The map started at Snow's Cut Bridge and ended at a place called Little Prong and a business named Sargasso Vineyards. The only other thing on the piece of paper was a name: Moody

Rawlins.

At first glance, Jeff thought nothing of this. Cash liked wine although he had to admit that her appreciation of it had never yet included North Carolina's offerings. But boutique vineyards were springing up every year. She may well have asked Tally to check this one out. Still, he memorized the map and headed back to the boat.

At that same moment, 55 miles away, Junior Fiske was picking up Tallahassee Bodine to head back to Carolina Beach. And they had news. Unnoticed by either man as they drove by was Cassandra Quick, in her bland tan Toyota Celica, who pulled out a bit behind them to follow them as they headed back to the coast.

———————————————————

Stella Conroy and I were getting out of her Mustang convertible at 4 o'clock in the afternoon. We were parked on Market in downtown Wilmington between 2nd and 3rd Streets and headed for a live music venue admirably named "The Blue Eyed Muse." Downtown Wilmington was not necessarily welcoming to visitors due to its one way streets, the poor condition of those streets, the narrowness of some venues, the often closed streets due to filming of television shows and movies, and the congestion of many streets as the city grew ever larger. But it was pleasant on the eye and a good deal of its architecture was both attractive and protected. At the moment, I was squinting and trying to avoid a headache because I had forgotten to put on my sunglasses and the bright summer sun blinded me for a moment.

"Hot as hell," Stella said as we headed for the door. "Ninety five and rising right off the pavement."

I looked at the big old building as we approached it. "What was this place in a previous incarnation," I asked her.

"Ziggy's—a popular nightclub. Now it's a music hall. Lotta live shows. Probably the best showcase for music in this entire state."

"No," I said "I mean originally. What was it?"

"Oh who remembers," Stella said. "Ask Big Daddy. He'll know. He reads history like I read the Raleigh News and Observer."

Big Daddy Washington and Stella and I were enjoying a kind of cease-fire, which is another way of saying that because he helped us on a previous case, Stella tries to ignore the fact that he is a major drug lord on Wilmington's north side. Sometimes she manages this. Other times she doesn't. So I always keep my gun readily available in case it's needed to quell a modern day version of the O.K. Corral. The door to the establishment was open, and when we walked in it was well-lit but empty, except for a few workers getting ready for the evening show. I saw Big Daddy a few feet down to the left of us. We headed over that way.

Today, I soon learned, was going to be a coping day. As we approached Big Daddy, Stella said to his two ginormous cousins, King Kong and Moses, who are usually at his side as bodyguards,

"Afternoon, boys. Please do not grope me. Y'all just know that would not work out well. And I won't shoot anyone. Scout's honor."

"Hello, Stella," Big Daddy said. "Cash, it's good to see you again." I nodded and smiled as the two of us sat down. It always surprises me that this handsome, sophisticated, well-educated and articulate man makes his money the way he does. But a lot of things surprise me.

"What's on your minds?" he asked.

"Who do you know in Sampson County might could get us a line on a guy we're lookin' for over around Ivanhoe," Stella said to him.

"Why? Are you chasing him?" Big Daddy's face showed the beginnings of a frown.

"No," I said quickly. "The spooks are chasing him. We need to find him to protect him."

Big Daddy Washington's eyes lost their focus as he sat back in his chair and didn't say anything. What filled the silence was a soprano voice singing a strong melody. I looked toward the stage at the front of the theater.

"Who's singing?" I asked.

Big Daddy smiled. "Tift Merritt," he said. "'Broken Hearted Men'. It's one of her best. Sorry. She distracts me. Sampson County. Ivanhoe. Do I want to know why they're chasing him?"

"No," said Stella.

"Very well," he said. "I have two people you should chat with. The first is probably the best, but he may know nothing about this. The second will do legwork that the first would not consider. If it comes to that, tell him I said to do it gratis. Got a pen? I'll write the information down for you. Moses, get me something to write on." When Moses handed him a sheet of paper, Big Daddy scribbled some names, addresses, and cell phone numbers on it and handed it to me.

"Voila," he said.

"Merci," I said.

"Later," Stella said.

Stella and I left the place as quietly as we'd entered. We were halfway home when I remembered that I'd wanted to know what the beautiful music hall now known as the Blue Eyed Muse had originally been built to house. I hoped it wasn't a detention center.

"I am in desperate need," Junior Fiske said to Tallahassee Bodine, "of a freezing glass of beer. And I mean freezing."

"I got me a twelve pack of beer in the Sawtelle's old freezer, Junior," Tally said. "We can drink it as it thaws. I'll boil some shrimps in lemon and garlic and hot sauce too."

"Yessir," Junior said. "Five minutes from now nirvana awaits us!"

At the stop light on the Wilmington side of Snow's Cut Bridge, the orange Kia headed into the turning left lane and activated its blinker signal. Cassandra Quick realized she was going to nearly reach the car while it waited for the light. So she quickly calculated her chances of being spotted and decided they were more than good. As the Kia idled at the red light, she donned a pair of sunglasses and pulled alongside it, heading over the bridge. Neither Junior nor Tally paid her the slightest bit of attention. A minute later, Junior made the turn while Cassandra headed into Carolina Beach. She figured she could do a u-turn at the first light that allowed it, and retrace her steps back over the bridge to try to find the two men she had been following.

CHAPTER TWELVE

Sheriff Billy Conroy was looking over some proposed plea deals that the Brunswick County District Attorney had recently shipped to him, when his private cell phone rang. He debated whether or not to answer it, thinking it would be Stella and he could call her later, but changed his mind after five rings.

"Conroy," he said.

"Billy, it's Buzz Chance from Horry County calling," said the voice on the other end of the phone.

"Well, well, well. Long time no hear, partner. What's happenin' down there in the deep red South? Crime draggin' y'all down?"

"Nope. Just the usual suspects," Chance said and chuckled. "Bunch of stupid country boys thinkin' they can be the next big thing by breakin' into cars and the like. But that ain't why I called. I'm curious. Have y'all had a visit from feds or the State Police lately lookin' for a guy?"

Billy Conroy sat up ramrod straight in his chair and tried to quickly figure out what and how much he wanted to say to his old friend. He chose instead to try to get Buzz Chance to tell him more of what he knew. So he said offhandedly,

"No. Why? Or didn't they tell you."

"Well, I got no specifics. But I did get a sizable impression they were talkin' about something pretty big. If I had to guess, they're looking for at least a serial burglar or rapist. Or, for that matter, a kidnapper or murderer even. Anyhow, they left me a photo. Truth is I ain't never seen the guy once. So I thought I'd call you. You're always into sheep dip up to and includin' your knees."

"Not this time, Buzz," Billy said good-naturedly. "But I will most assuredly call you if I do hear anything."

When Billy Conroy put his cell phone back on his desk he turned in his chair to glance out of the big picture window in his office that overlooked a well-tended flower garden and some fat healthy sago palms. He was hoping to see his pair of mated Cardinals. But they weren't around at the moment. Instead, the gray squirrels were running amuck among the palms.

"Louise," he hollered. "You there?"

"Where else would I be Billy" Louise hollered back. Five seconds later she stuck her head in the door. "What's up?"

"Let's leave now, go catch drinks and dinner at Mr. Ps. Y'all have been wantin' some of that underground tuna and I want a hunk of rare prime rib."

"Something on your mind?"

"Probably. But that don't preclude us enjoyin' ourselves, now does it?"

———————————————————

Darius Millar was getting ready to close up shop for the day at Mickey Huntley's Law Office when the front door opened and the Sheriff of New Hanover County walked in. This, in and of itself, was an unusual occurrence. Darius tried and failed to figure out what such an unscheduled visit might portend. The law and his boss were often at odds. She was, after all, a highly successful defense attorney.

"Is she in?" the Sheriff asked. He was in a pair of chinos and a black tee shirt. His feet were in a pair of mahogany loafers and he had forgone socks. If you didn't know him to see him, he'd have passed for a tourist.

"Just got back from errands, myself," Darius lied with a smile. "Let me check."

"No need to ruffle feathers," the man said. "I'm not here as an adversary."

"Be right back," Darius said and hustled into Mickey's private sanctum.

The lawyer was working on a brief when Darius approached her desk. He cleared his throat to announce himself. Mickey didn't look up.

"I told you don't bother me, Darius. I meant it." she said without inflection. "This voter suppression case is a fucking nightmare to win in this state with this Republican legislature. Facts have never mattered to Republicans, and now is not an exception to that truth."

"New Hanover Sheriff's outside." Darius said evenly. "He wants to talk with y'all."

Mickey Huntley abruptly stopped what she'd been doing and quickly looked at her assistant. "Why?" she asked.

"Don't know except he said it wasn't adversarial."

"That's what he always says when what he wants is access to some information he thinks I might have."

"Yes," Darius said. "You want me to stay to witness?"

"Of course." Mickey Huntley sighed deeply, stood up and walked to the small nicely appointed bar that was well-stocked, at the back of the room. She poured herself two fingers of bourbon, looked out her office window, saluted the busy waterfront street below, and downed the drink.

"Show him in," she said. She remained standing where she was, with her back to the door. What she heard next was this voice:

"Sorry to arrive unannounced, Counselor," Sheriff Wayne Pinckney said. "I just need a minute of your time."

Mickey Huntley turned and looked at the man for a moment before she answered him. "How may I help you, Sheriff," she said quietly.

"What do you know about the presence of a freight train load of federal officers crawling all over this and surrounding counties," he asked. "Supposedly looking for some sort of criminal."

Mickey Huntley had spent a lifetime controlling her facial muscles. They once again did not betray her. "Federal officers?" she asked. "Here?"

"Here and all over southeastern North Carolina," he said. "Probably parts of South Carolina as well."

"Who? FBI? Homeland Security? And by the way, Wayne," she said calmly, "if your inference that I would know anything is due to my occupation, you should know by now that your question offends me."

"Nothing's further from my mind, Mickey," he said easily. "It's just you hear things I don't so I thought I'd check. I want a true perspective. And no, it's neither one of those organizations you mentioned. It's CIA."

"And they came to you? For what? Cooperation?"

"More of a reasonably polite hands off don't mess with us sort of message. They didn't want or ask for any help. I guess they're going all out to find a rogue agent, or something like that, anyway. The head of the whole shebang's a woman: Beatrice Bush. She's got a suite at the Hilton on the Riverfront."

"Interesting," said Mickey Huntley. "But I can't help you, Wayne. I haven't heard a thing. If I do, I'll get in touch."

"Appreciate it," Sheriff Wayne Pinckney said. "Nice to see y'all again." And with that, he was gone.

For some moments, Mickey Huntley stood silently, leaning both of her hands on her desk. When she did look up, she still remained silent.

"Boss?" Darius Millar said softly.

Mickey let her gaze wander until she finally saw her assistant's face. "Want me to see is she home or what?" he said to the lawyer. She nodded.

The second his finger hit speed dial on his new cell phone, the rings began. After four rings, a voice said, "Do not dare to tell me that my workaholic partner is once again skipping dinner because some idiot has proposed another asinine bill and she has to go to Raleigh for a protest march. I will consider that excuse entirely unacceptable."

"Nothin' like that, Miss Sarah," Darius said. "She wants to talk with y'all 'bout somethin'. Here she is."

"Do you have any idea where Cash and Stella are," Mickey asked without benefit of a greeting.

"Why are you using Darius's phone," Sarah said quickly in response. "Something the matter with your private line?"

"I don't know. Probably not."

"I see. Well, Cash is in the shower at the moment and Stella's brought two dozen ears of corn and t-bones for the grill. I've made a huge salad with everything imaginable in it. Dinner's at eight thirty. All the boys are coming. Bring Darius if he wants to join us. We're also about to begin drinking sweet bourbon manhattans and getting a bit tipsy. So get a move on, baby. I miss you."

"Clock me. I'll be there in thirty minutes," the lawyer said.

CHAPTER THIRTEEN

I was pulling a pale yellow tank top over my head and tucking it into a pair of old Levi shorts I love, when Minerva strolled into my bedroom, sat down on a pretty area rug, wiggled her rump, and stared at me.

"Something on your mind," I said to her pleasantly. Her ears twitched and her tail started thump thump thumping on the rug. I bent to pick up the pair of leather sandals I have owned for eons and she wacked me lightly on the wrist with her right paw.

"You want an audience?" I asked. "I hope it doesn't involve your need to display your latest hunting trophy." Minerva likes to show off whatever she kills, and she kills with a sense of abandon. At that moment, Stella walked in carrying a drink that looked delicious.

"Who're y'all talking to," she said and handed me the drink.

"Minerva," I said and took a sip. I smacked my lips. "Yum. This is wonderful. What did you do, chip the ice?"

"Nope. I threw it in the blender along with the sweet vermouth and the cherry juice. Dilutes the cloying sweetness. Mickey just called Sarah who got the feeling that something more than dinner's on the Counselor's mind."

"Hardly unusual," I said, strapping on my sandals.

"She was in her back office," said Stella. "She borrowed Darius's phone to make the call. She wanted to know where you and I were." The two of us looked at each other. Stella smiled. Finally, I nodded.

"Okay," I said. "Let's wait to see what the lawyer has to say before we even try to finalize our conclusions."

"And the beat goes on…the beat goes on…" Stella sang that old Sixties tune and soft-shuffled out of my bedroom. When she was gone, Minerva glared at me. Then she opened her mouth and let loose a heart-stopping yowl that would frighten a zombie. I grinned at her.

"Something along those lines, you crazy cat," I said to her. She purred contentedly.

Minerva walked along with me as we ambled our way into the kitchen to join what turned out to be a rather eventful dinner party.

Anthony Sargasso was walking up the hill to the big white barn where his brother Paul was testing some of the cabernet grapes he grew for his own consumption. Anthony was excited. When he reached the barn door it was open and he could see his brother talking with Moody Rawlins in the back of the building, next to one of the wine storage vats. He quickly joined them.

"Yes indeed, boss," Moody was saying. "Them last two boys, I call 'em vanilla and licorice, was a good hire. Both work hard and they never complain. I'm hopin' to keep 'em both another year."

"I trust you don't call them that to their faces," Paul Sargasso said with a ghost of a smile on his lips. "Last thing we need is a lawsuit at our doorstep." Then he turned and greeted his brother warmly. "Hello, Tony. What's new?"

Before answering his brother, Anthony looked pointedly at Moody Rawlins.

"Boss," Moody Rawlins said somewhat hurriedly, "y'all don't need me anymore, I'll just be headin' home. OK?" Anthony waited until the man was out of earshot.

"I finally found my assistant," his brother said. "She starts on Monday and she's perfect. She's even interested enough in what I'm doing to be willing to experiment with variant strains in case of any upcoming legal difficulties."

"As in…" Paul said.

"As in if my current offerings were to become ATF classified and I had to abandon them," Anthony said.

"Ah hah," his brother said. "And that is almost more than I need to know, little brother. Care to join me in a glass of my reserve cabernet?"

Cassandra Quick had been parked for more than an hour, and she was getting restless. She was sitting in her car along a little countryside road waiting for something to happen, because when she'd retraced her steps to where she'd last seen the orange Kia, this is where she found it. It was situated in front of a huge old barn that looked as though it would collapse if you so much as sneezed at it.

And she was beginning to think that these two odd men were nothing more than what they looked to be: grape pickers; probably migrants. For all she knew, they could have simply been out looking around their new environment at the Sargasso Estate and didn't pose a threat to anyone, let alone to her and her cousin Cuddy.

She looked at her watch and decided to give it fifteen more minutes, and at that precise moment the two men she'd been following made an appearance. Although she was behind the cover of a lot of thick shrubbery and parked across the road from them, she suddenly worried she'd be spotted. But neither guy looked her way. The fat guy driving did a u-turn and headed back towards the intersection. She waited to start her car until they were a fair distance ahead of her.

This time the orange Kia turned left at the light and headed over Snow's Cut Bridge into the heart of Carolina Beach. Cassandra made the light and followed it. When they both hit the red light at Cape Fear Boulevard, the Kia switched into the inside lane and turned it's blinker on. Finally, at Carolina Beach Avenue, it turned right, heading south. At another left, the Kia went toward the Atlantic Ocean on a street named Beach House Lane. Cassandra realized this was a short street. She stopped just after she'd turned, and pulled alongside what looked to be an abandoned cottage.

The orange Kia pulled into a paved drive meant for parking, and the two men emerged and walked right into the house without even knocking. Thirty seconds later, a woman walked out of the cottage carrying a platter of meat. She headed around the parked cars and disappeared in front of the place. Then another woman emerged carrying two bottles of beer and two drinks on a tray. She too disappeared from view. They're having a cookout, Cassandra said to herself. What she said next to her cousin Cuddy as she voice dialed his number would take this particular situation into totally uncharted territory.

Maurice "Big Daddy" Washington had stayed successful in a difficult business because he had an acute sense of curiosity. So after his meeting with Stella Conroy and Cash Delaney, he thought about their rather odd request and the reason for it, and finally decided to find out what was really going on. His call was made on a prepaid phone to a trusted informant of his, working the police beat in the city of Wilmington.

"Homer," the guy said who answered.

"What's going on with the spooks in town," Big Daddy said. "Why're they here?"

"A guy got away from them," Homer said. "Street says he killed a muckety-muck and they're hellacious pissed."

"We know who?"

"No idea. Ain't no how related to our side of the street, boss."

"I never know what is and is not related, Homer. That's why I crave information that I pay a lot for. Find out what is what, who they're chasing, why they're chasing, what—if anything—it has to do with Ivanhoe, and get back to me. Two days be good."

"I'm on it," said Homer.

"Keep me informed," Big Daddy said.

"Always," Homer answered. "I hear, you hear."

———————————————————

Billy Conroy and Louise Dickson were enjoying a very pleasant evening at Mr. Ps. They had run into a bunch of their friends and the mutual repartee had been fast and funny. The drinks had been generous and when they sat down to dinner the food had been superb. Over some strong brewed coffee and dishes of blueberry cobbler, Billy said to her,

"That CIA mess with Stella and Cash and the corpse?"

Louise looked sharply at him. "What about it, Billy. We're hands off."

"I guess I need to make positive on that. Buzz Chance called me today wantin' to know did I hear anything about CIA agents swarming all over southeastern North Carolina and northwestern South Carolina. I've got to satisfy my worried mind that the girls are truly out of it. Neither one of them is suitable for a federal prison, and my daughter would actually go insane."

"They're working on that Sargasso thing aren't they? It's why we deputized them."

"Theoretically, yes," Billy said. "Years of knowing my daughter better than anybody—and that includes her husband—tells me I need to make sure. Do y'all mind drivin' to Carolina Beach when we're finished here?"

"Of course not. But if, for whatever reason, they aren't, then what?" asked Louise.

"I need to try my best to change their minds," Sheriff Billy Conroy said.

Fifteen minutes later, they were headed to the cottage on Beach House Lane.

CHAPTER FOURTEEN

Eric Malanga was looking forward to walking to Jacksonville, where Camp Lejeune was located. He had decided to take his time and to stop and enjoy what beauty the back roads and wild fields and small towns in North Carolina would offer him. He had found a backpack abandoned at the local dump and filled it the morning of his trip with a change of clothes, water, some jerky and rolls from a nearby store, a bag of blueberries, a thin blanket, a book on the state's warblers, and another on its flowers. He wore his binoculars around his neck. He had stuffed fifty dollars in his pocket from what was left of the money he'd recovered from his safe deposit box when he'd reentered the United States from Myanmar. Now, he thought grimly, reclaimed as Burma.

If he had chosen to power walk the trip he could have made it in one twenty-four-hour period with intermittent periods of rest. His training as a marine would have made this easily possible. But Eric was no longer in a hurry. Neither was he unaware of the panic his very existence on American soil may well have triggered in the CIA. But he was philosophical about it. They would do whatever they would do. And so would he. Eric knew this as his existential moment and he would see it through to its conclusion. His death no longer interested him. Too much of him had already died.

When he noticed a road sign that read "Wallace" five miles, he knew he was walking into Pender County. So he decided to stop at the small park he found that welcomed visitors and was located on the outskirts of this small town. Perhaps he'd discover some beautiful birds, or even watch a few innings of a teenage baseball game. He'd been a damn good pitcher in his high school years.

When he reached the park, he headed for the restrooms to clean up and when he'd finished he took a seat at a table not far from the center of the park where a bunch of folks were exercising their dogs. He decided to see if he could spot a bluebird, or perhaps a thrush, or even a towhee. He aimed his binoculars at a large stand of pine threes to the left of him and scanned the trees. The first bird he saw was one he did not expect to see and it delighted him. It was a prothonotary warbler with a vivid yellow breast and it was singing its song on one of the tall pine's highest branches. Eric Malanga was enchanted. A few minutes later, he spotted a nest with a bluebird. Then he watched as its mate landed on the rim of the nest carrying worms in its beak. Then, of course, he heard the squawks of little baby bluebirds, and the feeding ritual began in earnest. At that moment, Eric realized he, too, was hungry.

He took four good-sized pieces of beef jerky, one roll, a bottle of water and a handful of blueberries for his lunch. As he was finishing his meal, a boy about five years old approached him.

"Hi," was what the boy said. His voice was light and breathless as though he had been running.

Eric Malanga looked down at the child and smiled. "Hi yourself, young man," he said. "That's quite a tee shirt you're wearing."

"Y'all like it," the kid said and beamed.

"I do indeed," Eric said. It was a bright orange shirt with this inscription in white lettering: IMPEACH THIS PRESIDENT. There was a graphic of a fat man with a huge butt swinging a golf club at broken White House windows behind the message.

"My mom's a Democratic woman," the boy said proudly. "She hates him. So I help her out when I wear this tee shirt."

At that moment, a tall, lanky, pretty brunette in her early thirties reached the boy, put a hand on his narrow shoulder, and said "My son Daniel isn't always aware of the old dictum never talk to strangers." She said this without the slightest bit of emotion but then, Eric thought, she didn't have to.

"Yes," he said. "Well, your son and I were discussing politics. He's supportive of your views."

If this reasonable response startled the woman, she gave no hint of it. "He's supportive of whatever he thinks will get him an extra hour of action on Play Station," she said. But then she smiled. "Do you live in Wallace?"

"I live by the river outside Ivanhoe," Eric said. "I'm a sort of naturalist. I like to walk and study and interact with birds and plants and other things in nature that might, of course, kill me, but wish me no harm."

The woman looked at him and because Eric Malanga was used to silence and appraisal he let her look. Then she said, "'Might possibly drown me but wills me no ill.' That's a line from one of our most enduring poets, Edna St. Vincent Millay. We do ourselves a monumental disservice by neglecting the truths our poets offer us. Would you like to join my son and me before returning to your journey? We're going to get an ice cream at the snow cone shop at the other end of the park."

"I'll walk with you," Eric Malanga said. "It's on my way."

"I want cherry with hot fudge and marshmallow in a big dish," exclaimed the boy named Daniel who was wearing the bright orange tee shirt that called for the impeachment of an American President in the year of our Lord 2018.

———————————————

"So there I was not more than 300 feet away from the house when who walks out of it? Stella Conroy." Cassandra Quick said to her cousin Cuddy. "And if that doesn't get your attention, this next one will fry your eyes. Who followed her? None other than Attorney Mickey Huntley. That's the house those two men went to, and what they appear to be doin' now is having a cookout. I don't know what the hell to do. But something is goin' on. This is no coincidence."

"Jesus. Mickey Huntley's a legal pistol. And Stella Conroy," Cuddy said. "She's the Sheriff's daughter, right?"

"Exactly right." said Cassandra. "But she's also a private detective. Got an office here in Carolina Beach. Has had for years. I heard she took a partner a while ago. Don't know who."

"It don't matter who," Cuddy said. "Don't you kinda sorta know the daughter?"

"Say hi to passing on the street," Cassandra said. "She solved that murder a few years ago; the one involved a Lumbee warrior's son. Conroy proved him innocent. She's an honorary Lumbee now."

"Maybe that's our way in," Cuddy said. "We could feel her out by telling at least a part of the story. See if she'll tell us what if anything she's doing. Y'all get what I mean? Or we could just choose to trust that Mickey Huntley's involvement coincides with ours and tell her flat out what's on our minds. She's a pistol but she shoots straight."

"I'll think on it," said Cassandra. "Meantime, I'm intending to wait until it gets dark, see if I can get close enough to overhear anything they're talking about. I'll be in touch." As she broke the call to her cousin, Cassandra calculated she'd have another 45 minutes of sitting and watching before the sun finally set.

Brooke Malanga was restless. She knew she wanted to do something about this mess with her brother Eric. She just had no idea what she should or shouldn't do. The last thing she wanted was to attract the attention of the CIA again. That organization frightened her. But surely there was something she could do. She hadn't heard word one from those private detectives she'd hired, and her hopes of a resolution were dimming daily. She considered calling them when her cell phone rang.

"This is Brooke," she said.

"Brooke, this is Mickey Huntley. Are you busy at the moment or can you join me for dinner in Carolina Beach." Brooke was momentarily stunned. She'd just been thinking about the situation and then her phone rang. She filed the coincidence under Karma and said,

"It'll take me an hour to get there."

"That's fine. Dinner's at eight thirty. The house is the last one on Beach House Lane. It borders the Atlantic."

"I'll find it," Brooke Malanga said. "My GPS hasn't failed me yet. I hope there's news."

"Of a sort," the lawyer said; and then Brooke heard the click on her phone that ended the call. Although that last response from her attorney was not what Brooke Malanga would have called positive news, it was something. So this was how she chose to view it. She grabbed her purse, her keys, and her sunglasses and headed to her car to make the trip to Carolina Beach and an evening dinner beside the Atlantic Ocean.

CHAPTER FIFTEEN

Twenty minutes into Cassandra Quick's wait for sunset, four women walked out of the cottage on Beach House lane, turned to their left and headed straight for Cassandra and her car: Stella Conroy, Mickey Huntley and two others she'd never seen before. They weren't saying anything until they were nearly up to Cassandra's parked car. Then, Mickey Huntley began to speak. She looked animated. The group of four stopped walking.

What the hell what the hell what the hell, Cassandra thought to herself. She quickly decided to roll her window down, grab the newspaper on her passenger seat, leave her sunglasses on and see what she could learn about this situation, if anything. This is what she heard.

"So Brooke is joining us for dinner," Mickey Huntley was saying. "She'll be here in a half hour or so. But you two need to know that the CIA is out in force all over southeastern North Carolina and northeastern South Carolina. They're visiting law enforcement and every post office, looking for someone who has actually seen her brother."

"Well shit," Stella Conroy said. "We asked that same question a while ago in the Ivanhoe post office. Guy there said he was certain Malanga did not live in that town."

"Jesus Christ," a tall, tanned, and dark-haired redhead said. "The minute they hit Ivanhoe we'll be facing serious consequences."

"I understand that, Sarah," Mickey Huntley said calmly. "But Brooke can protect us if she chooses to do it. I need deniability, and she can provide it simply by saying she hired Cash and Stella to look for her long-lost brother, not telling either one of them who he really is. It's perfectly plausible she'd do that anyway because most people who are not completely and utterly reckless would refuse to help her if they knew the real circumstances."

"We're not completely reckless, Mickey," the woman who was probably Stella's business partner with the odd name of Cash said. "Stella and I delegate when we can, which is why we sent Tally and Junior over to Sargasso's estate to find out what's really going on over there."

Mickey Huntley looked at her. "Do I need to know about this?" she asked.

"No," Stella said. "It's just about drugs that Sargasso's brother is manufacturing and selling, that probably aren't yet illegal but that we figure someone's child died or lost his mind or was physically incapacitated after swallowing whatever the hell it is. Daddy's gonna take care of it when we're finished investigating. Although truthfully, it's not hard to sympathize with whoever is goin' after Sargasso. But when harassment turns to destruction of property, there's consequences."

"Girls," a male voice shouted. "I'm getting ready to put the steaks on."

"I assume the boys know nothing of any this." Mickey Huntley said.

"No," Stella said. "But we can let Tally and Junior give us the latest on the Sargasso investigation. I don't know what the hell's gonna break loose once Brooke gets here. Cooper will be furious. Jefferson will be apoplectic."

"I'll meet her outside to alert her that mum's the word until they're gone. How you get rid of Coop and Jeff for the evening is your business," Mickey said.

"And I'll take a look to see what I can find about the progress they're making with this blanket approach to finding out where Eric Malanga is," the redhead said. "Might take me a few hours tonight, but rest assured Beatrice Bush definitely uses email."

And with that, the four women started walking back to the cottage on Beach House Lane. Never once did they notice or speak to Cassandra Quick who, at this particular moment, was stunned by all she'd overheard.

On the afternoon that Eric Malanga was chatting with the boy Daniel in the orange tee shirt, two deputies from the Pender County Sheriff's Office were on patrol in Rocky Point, a town in the county that is occasionally a target for tornadoes in southeastern North Carolina. It had been a quiet day. On their dashboard was a photo of a man in uniform that the Sheriff had told them to be on the lookout for. He had issued the BOLO to all law enforcement agencies throughout the county, despite the fact that he had not been asked to do this by the CIA, the federal agency overseeing this manhunt. As the two deputies approached the first of two stoplights in the town, one said to the other,

"Let's grab lunch at McDonald's. I ain't had a double cheeseburger in a while."

"Shake and fries be good too," his partner said.

"Damn straight."

Once the two deputies had their order in hand, they walked to one of the outside tables to enjoy it. They were finishing up their lunch when the one facing the street said, "Take a look at the guy walking down the street; he's passing the drugstore right about now."

As his partner turned to look, the man in question opened the door of a fairly new automobile, seated himself, started the car and pulled away. He was headed north. "Yeah, I see the resemblance," the partner said. 'Think we ought to follow?"

"I sure as hell do," said the deputy who had first noticed the man. "We find this guy the feds are looking for, we're golden. Might even be enough to land us a promotion and a raise. Maybe even get an interview on Fox News. Let's go."

Just outside of Rocky Point, the man in the fairly new automobile hooked onto Route 40 and increased his speed accordingly. The two deputies saw this and did the same. "Let's see where he's going," the deputy who was driving said. "For all we know, he may be thinkin' on killing somebody else and is on his way to do it."

"If it's him," his partner said, pointing at the photo on the dashboard.

"If it ain't him, I'll eat my hat," the one driving said.

His partner guffawed and said, "That I would pay to see."

This tableau, an unsuspecting stranger driving north while being followed by a sheriff's patrol car, continued until the man in the fairly new automobile arrived at the tiny one-stoplight town of Wallace. When the stranger came to the stoplight he turned right, heading east on Route 11. The sheriff's patrol car did the same. After going about 10 miles, the deputy driving the patrol car said,

"Time to pull him over. "He's headed straight for Camp Lejeune."

Once he'd said this, he activated the patrol car's siren.

Thirty seconds later, the stranger driving the fairly new automobile pulled to the side of the road and looked behind him at the two deputies walking toward him. Then, he got out of the car and began to close the car door. As he did so, he turned and smiled at the deputies.

"Put your hands where I can see them," shouted the deputy who had driven the patrol car. "Do it now!" Both he and his partner had drawn their weapons and aimed them at the man.

"What's the problem, officer," the man said amiably. "I'm just on my way home, I wasn't speeding, and there's nothing wrong with my car. It was just inspected last week. Here, let me show you some identifi…" and the man reached inside his jacket pocket. Those were the last words that the man driving the fairly new automobile ever uttered. Both sheriff deputies shot him at the same time and each hit him three times as he fell face first against his automobile and then crumpled to the ground.

The two deputies looked at each other. Both of them were sweating and both were momentarily unable to move. Then the one driving nodded to his partner and the two of them cautiously approached the dead body that had recently been alive. Once they reached him, the driver poked him. The body turned slightly but rolled back. The partner reached down and turned the dead man over. His eyes were wide open and the look on his face signaled surprise. There were six bullet holes in the man's chest. Any one of them would have proved fatal. The deputy who had rolled him reached into the inside pocket of the man's jacket and retrieved a brown leather wallet. It was slim and looked expensive.

After studying the driver's license and credit cards and other odds and ends he found, the deputy looked at his partner and said, "We just killed an active duty marine on his way home to Camp Lejeune. His name's Joseph Thomas. Got a wife and four little ones. Better grab that photo on the dash. We need to see is he the one they're lookin' for."

When the two deputies looked at the dead man and then looked at the photograph, they finally looked at each other. There was a resemblance but that was all it was. This was not the man the feds were trying to find and capture. By now, traffic had slowed and several cars had pulled off the road. A voice from one of the stopped cars yelled,

"Everything all right over there? Y'all need help?"

"We're fine. Nothing to see here folks. Please move along." The deputy who'd been driving turned and waved the passing and stopped cars on. In a few minutes, traffic returned to normal and the deputies had covered the body with a blanket.

"What the hell are we gonna do now," the deputy holding the wallet said.

"We gotta call the sheriff," his partner said. "We had reason to believe he was the hunted man. We stopped him. And as we approached, he made a move we both saw as reaching for a weapon. We shot in self-defense. You know the sheriff'll back us."

"It ain't the sheriff worries me," said the other deputy. "It's the feds."

As his partner dialed his cell phone, which gave him a direct line to the sheriff, a sudden flash of a huge hawk, diving directly on a target in a nearby field, hit their vision. Both men flinched. A few minutes later, the deputy making the call clicked off his phone and said to his partner,

"Sheriff's on his way. He's bringing a wagon. Gonna take a while so we might as well sit in the car, turn the AC on. This heat's a bitch."

Once back in the car, the deputy still holding the thin leather wallet said, "Don't think I forgot. I want to be there, you eat your hat for dinner."

CHAPTER SIXTEEN

Eric Malanga rounded a curve on Route 11 that would eventually get him to Camp Lejeune and saw, some distance ahead, a Sheriff's patrol car with two deputies inside and their car running. He stopped in his tracks. Then he saw a second car and what could be a body covered by a blanket just ahead of the running patrol car. He quickly turned to his left and entered the shelter of a good sized copse of fir trees, which made him invisible to the road traffic as well as to the two men ahead of him.

He chose a circle of grass to sit on and began to ponder the scene ahead of him, finally deciding that whatever it was he did not want to become involved. Too much risk. So he leaned against a small oak tree, lifted his binoculars, and scanned the trees for birds and the ground for indigenous wild plants. As he was watching two hawks circling an open field further inside his location, a siren became audible. In a few minutes, a sheriff's car arrived and pulled alongside the car where the two men were sitting. Minutes later, what people used to call a wagon for the dead pulled behind the parked patrol car. This vehicle was a coroner's station wagon.

Eric Malanga decided he wanted to try to hear what was being said so he walked noiselessly behind the cover of the fir tree copse until he could faintly discern men's voices. But he could not get close enough to overhear this conversation.

"…were pretty damn sure, sir." One of the two deputies who had been sitting in the parked car said.

"Pretty damned sure don't even cut the bait this time, boys, let alone catch the fish," a man who looked like he might be the sheriff said. "This fella don't look to be more than a third cousin of our man. The CIA's gonna fry my balls and eat 'em for breakfast. Y'all get the heavy drift that's attached to this particular incident?"

"Yessir," the two young deputies mumbled.

"All finished, sheriff," a guy from the coroner's station wagon hollered. "We'll meet you at the hospital morgue."

"I don't need a coroner to tell me the man's dead and he died from an overdose of bullets from these two boys state-issued guns. Tell whoever's acting coroner today at the hospital I'll be along in a while. I've got a few fences need mending," the sheriff said dyspeptically. Turning to his two deputies, he said, "I couldn't have dreamed up a worse nightmare than this if I'd soaked myself in rum and seen the snakes running haywire on the ceiling. Meet me back at the office. Do not dawdle."

When Big Daddy Washington's phone rang two days after he'd told his informant Homer to find out what was going on with the CIA agents crawling all over the area, he was sitting in his private backroom elegant office on Marstellar Street in downtown Wilmington; he was enjoying one of his favorite snacks of a dozen oysters on the half shell with lemon and hot sauce and a glass of white merlot, while counting receipts from the latest monthly sales at this sizable Antiques Emporium. The ringing of the phone annoyed him but he answered it.

"Talk to me," he said.

"Boss, this is Homer. You said two days. It's two days. I got some crazy motherfucking news."

"As in…" Big Daddy asked. He knew Homer had a penchant for the dramatic, mainly because he thought it promoted him in Big Daddy's eyes. Usually, it didn't. This time in retrospect it actually might have.

"As in I'm in Pender County talking with some bona fide sources looking to see what they might have heard and what comes over the police band radio?"

Big Daddy sighed. "Get to it Homer, please. I'm enjoying oysters and a glass of chilled semi-sweet wine."

"Two sheriff's deputies shot dead a guy they thought was who the CIA was lookin' for; turns out he's a married marine with four kids on his way home to Camp Lejeune. The sheriff must be goin' apeshit. He ain't said a word yet. But I expect he will next few hours. Whaddya want me to do?"

Big Daddy did a brief calculus of possibilities regarding what he'd just heard; then he made a decision and said, "Who does the street go to in the New Hanover County Sheriff's Office? Y'all up to speed?"

"I am," Homer said.

"Good. I need a name on this guy the CIA's hankering after and whatever else you can discover. Sooner the better."

"It'll cost," Homer said."

"Not a problem. We're good."

"Boss." Homer said. "I hear, you hear." And with that he ended the call.

I can't say that dinner was especially enjoyable that evening on Beach House Lane, because the majority of diners were all distracted by the need to be finished so the important work could begin. We did, however, manage to get through it without incident. Tally and Junior reported on their latest find: Anthony Sargasso was hiring a helper for his drug lab. Tally had sat a few feet from him as he ate his lunch in the vineyards and discussed the job requirements over his cell phone. This addition was no doubt due to his current monetary success, which was what we were hired to find out about and what we intended to put a stop to, whether by persuasion or leverage. Shortly after the main course, Tally and Junior left with instructions to keep an eye on Anthony Sargasso's activities.

Over dessert of lemon tarts and whipped cream, Cooper said to Stella, "You seem miles away from here this evening Stella. Something on your mind?"

"I was just thinking the same thing about every woman at this table, Coop," Jefferson Davis said. "What the hell's goin on with y'all? You jammed up again with trouble?"

"It's probably my…" Brooke Malanga started to say and stopped when her lawyer put a hand on her shoulder and squeezed a bit.

"Actually, we all are a bit distracted," Mickey Huntley said easily. "And I'm afraid it's my fault. Brooke is a new client of mine and I've asked Stella and Cash to meet with her after dinner. I've also asked Sarah to do some research on a project I'm working on. In both cases, I'm under a significant deadline. Consequently, so are the three of them."

"Well okay," Coop said. "Thanks for letting me know my intuition's still intact, Mick. The two of us will clean the grill and rake the beach and be on our way."

We all got up from dinner and while I was helping Sarah clear it, I noticed Jefferson looking intently at me. Then he slid his chair back against the table rim, leaned over to me, kissed me on the cheek and said, "I sincerely hope you are not once again up to no good by which I mean putting your life at significant risk for somebody else's pie-in-the-sky whim. I have zero interest in living my life without you."

I smiled at him but before I had a chance to answer, Billy Conroy and Louise Dickson opened the front door and looked around at the bunch of us.

"I want to talk with you two," Billy said to Stella and me. "And I won't take no for an answer."

I think my jaw dropped. I looked at Stella, whose face was rapidly turning scarlet. A sure sign her blood pressure was rising. "Not now, daddy," she said forcefully.

"Yes, now. Right goddamned now," her father said. Louise flinched at the tone of Billy's voice.

"Jesus Christ," said Sarah Ehrenson to nobody and everybody in particular.

At around five o'clock on the afternoon that the two Pender County deputies shot and killed an active duty marine they thought was the target of a CIA manhunt, Beatrice Bush was standing in front of a closet wearing only her underwear, in her suite at the Riverside Hilton. She was deciding what to wear for an early dinner. As she debated a black sheath versus a red pantsuit, her hotel phone rang.

"Yes," she said.

A man on the other end of the line cleared his throat before saying, "Uh, is this Agent Bush?"

"It is," she said. "And you are…"

"Sheriff Haskell Shorter, Pender County, ma'am."

"Yes, what can I do for you, sheriff?"

"Uh, well, it seems we got a bit of a dicey situation here, ma'am." The sheriff said.

"Sheriff Shorter, if this involves me or my agency, please get to whatever's on your mind. My patience is not unlimited."

"No ma'am. Mine neither. There's no good way to say this so here it is. Two of my deputies, with a BOLO on their dashboard, while on patrol shot and killed an active duty marine they thought was the guy y'all are looking for. I have got to make a statement about this sooner or later but first we got to notify family—he's got a wife and four young kids—and I need to hear from you on how y'all want to handle your end of things." Beatrice Bush was momentarily stunned. She felt as though she'd been sucker punched. After an interminable half minute of silence, she heard this ridiculous sheriff saying, "Ma'am? "Ma'am? Y'all there?"

For the first time in her life Agent Beatrice Bush was at a complete loss for words. She simply couldn't tell if she was all there or not. Finally, she managed, "Do nothing public, including notification of family, until I or one of my assistants notify you how to proceed. Understood?" When she heard a mumbled "Yes ma'am" she ended the phone call.

CHAPTER SEVENTEEN

Camp Lejeune is a 246-square-mile U.S. military training facility that is located in Jacksonville, North Carolina. To give you some perspective on the size of the base, the island of Manhattan is 22.7 square miles. To say that one could easily lose one's way on this military base is, therefore, a bit of an understatement. Currently, there are approximately 150,000 marines, dependents, and civilians residing at the camp. That number, of course, fluctuates due to deployments.

The main base gets support from six satellite facilities: the Marine Corps Air Station at New River, Stone Bay, Camp Johnson, Camp Geiger, Courthouse Bay, and the Greater Sandy Run Training Area. The base has its own housing for troops, its own K-12 school, its own hospital, and its own superstore commissary, as well as its own jail. There are fitness centers, recreation areas, movie theaters, legal assistance, veterinary services, marine marts, and parks. If you never left the camp throughout your entire enlistment, you would not want for a thing unless you wanted to gamble in a casino on your leave. For that you'd have to visit Virginia or cross North Carolina and spend your vacation at the Harrah's Cherokee Casino Resort outside Ashville.

Eric Malanga had not visited this marine base since his training there ended over a decade ago. During his time away, it had both grown and remained remarkably unchanged. The base's fourteen miles of beaches makes it a major area for amphibious assault training, and its location between two deep water ports of the cities of Wilmington and Morehead City allows for fast deployments. He knew these beaches well. So navigation itself would not be a problem. Successful illegal entry would be.

But he had no intention of trying to enter the facility illegally. He'd be turned away.

He intended to camp somewhere along the beach just outside of Jacksonville, because he knew where he could find the man he had traveled to see. Marines looked forward to weekends because their furloughs allow them to leave the base and spend some time in civvies; and they have a few favorite bars and grills where they are welcomed heartily by natives. Drinks are good, pool tables are busy, starchy food keeps most of them on the sane side of half-sober, and a lot of nubile girls and women enjoy their company. Eric was familiar with these places. So he picked a pretty little spot of beach with a half-circle of scrub oaks and a soft, low dune, and set up his camp. Tomorrow he'd walk into town in the afternoon and begin his search for Clay Carpenter, the man who had once declined to forward his desperate call for assistance.

Cudworth Sweat was sound asleep in one of Cassandra Quick's porch chairs when she pulled up and parked her car in front of her home in Elrod, North Carolina. It was closing in on midnight and Cassandra was so tired she thought about just sitting in her car and sleeping. But that was out of the question, because she knew she'd be unable to quiet her mind until she'd talked with Cuddy about what all she'd seen and heard this evening in Carolina Beach. So she struggled out her small car and walked up her three front steps where she nudged her cousin's right boot until he opened his eyes and looked at her.

"What's the time?" is what he said to her.

"Almost midnight," Cassandra said. "I need a coffee. Did you make any?"

"Pot's near full," he said. "Your eyes are tired. Sit and I'll make us a couple sweet tans."

"Lovely," she said.

A few minute later, Cuddy handed his cousin a steaming cup of French roast coffee that was heavy on the sugar and cream. The two of them sat awhile in silence and sipped the brew. Eventually, Cassandra said "Full moon tonight."

"I wondered about that," her cousin answered.

"Yes. And we have choices we must make. I thought on the myth of the moon rabbit while I drove here. If we decide wrong, a man will die. If we choose right, he will live with his scars much like the crane does. But I don't know if this man wishes to live or wishes to die."

"Cousin?"

"In early summer, during that week I visited my relatives in Ivanhoe, I was fishing on the Black River where I met a fellow angler. We exchanged pleasantries but believe me when I tell you he was a broken man. Not physically. He was a beautiful physical specimen. But emotionally he was half dead. His sorrow owned his heart. I never learned his name and he never learned mine. But he did tell me he has a camp outside of town on a bit of raw land that fronts the river. We could find it if we looked."

"This is what you learned this evening?" her cousin interjected.

Cassandra Quick sighed. "I learned so much I'm on overload. I'm trying to tell you in my own way, cousin. Will you bear with me?"

"I'm chastened," Cuddy said. "Please..."

"The CIA is here in our territory, all over it actually, and actively looking to kill this man," she said. "They believe he murdered one of their own. I don't believe they are correct. The man I spoke with isn't a murderer. I saw his soul. He's non-violent. He's worthy of life, not death. Stella Conroy and her partner with the strange name of Cash are looking for him. And the CIA may be about to discover this and they both have been warned, ordered really, to remain uninvolved. But they are also simultaneously tracking the disturbances at Sargasso Industries, so we are facing some more immediate choices and we may well be in danger of discovery ourselves."

"How do they know about Sargasso?"

"Billy Conroy must have asked them to look into it. He probably deputized them. Those two men you saw the other night are their eyes and ears. They're plants and both are working at the vineyard. And in the midst of it all is the formidable Mickey Huntley who remains at present superbly adroit at keeping the entire mess afloat."

Cudworth Sweat sat forward in the porch chair and cleared his throat. When he spoke, Cassandra had to lean in to hear him. "We need to sleep on this. We can't make these kinds of dangerous decisions in a rush."

"Yes. You're right. And you'll sleep here," she said. "But when it's morning we'll need to be decisive. I don't believe there's much time to waste in either case."

Fifteen minutes later, Cassandra Quick was asleep in her bed. Her cousin Cuddy had chosen the living room floor with a blanket and a pillow. He was used to things that did not give against his weight.

At five thirty in the evening on the day two sheriff's deputies shot dead an active marine sergeant in Pender County, North Carolina, Agent Bart Clarkson was sitting in Alfredo's Italian Restaurant in Clinton, North Carolina, enjoying a dry gin martini with three olives. He had been on the road in Sampson County most of the day visiting post office after post office, in hopes of finding someone who had recently seen rogue operative Eric Malanga. No one had.

So he had stopped his inquiries for the day, booked a room at a Comfort Inn in Clinton, and found this restaurant to enjoy a few drinks and some dinner.

A pleasant-looking waitress smiled at him as she began to serve the beginnings of his meal. He'd ordered a shrimp cocktail with a small loaf of garlic bread for an appetizer and when she looked at his nearly empty martini glass he nodded his head, saying, "Tell the bartender he's good at dry martinis and that I'll have another. When my entrée comes, I'll also have a carafe of your house merlot."

Fifteen minutes later, he was served a large rare cut of prime rib with a generous side of linguini in a garlic butter sauce, and a green salad with blue cheese dressing. The wine was fruity and semi-dry and, to his surprise, he enjoyed it. He was getting a credit card out of his wallet to pay for his meal when his cell phone rang. One glance told him it was Beatrice Bush on the line.

"Evening Boss," he said.

"Where are you?" she said.

"Place called Clinton in Sampson County. I've been in the county all day. Nothing's materialized so far. But I've got the rest of the county tomorrow. One place with about three hundred inhabitants is called Ivanhoe. Can you just imagine? Shades of King Arthur's Court."

"Forget about Ivanhoe," she said. "Are you close to Pender

County?"

"It's right next door. Why?"

"I need you to get over to the sheriff's office ASAP. That's in Burgaw."

Bart Clarkson felt his adrenaline kick in right before he said to his boss, "What's going on, Bea?"

"Two Sheriff's deputies shot an active duty marine to death because they thought he was Eric Malanga."

Clarkson felt his jaw swing so loose he thought he might have unhinged it. Finally, he managed, "How could that happen? Why were they even aware of Malanga?"

"Sheriff Redneck Numbnuts issued a BOLO to all of them with the old photo of Malanga we gave to him."

"Jesus fucking Christ," Bart Clarkson muttered, just as the waitress reached to remove his dinner plate. The young women blanched, grabbed his plate, and scurried away.

"Yes," Bea said. "And now we've got to try to fix it somehow."

"Can't be done," he said softly. "It may be an accident but it's still murder."

"Well, something has to be done. I am on my way to Burgaw now. I'll be getting there in forty five minutes give or take. I want you to meet me."

"It'll take me closer to an hour but I'll be there as quickly as I can."

"Good. I instructed the sheriff to do nothing until we get there."

"Okay. I'll see you soon. Drive safe." But Beatrice Bush had already ended the call.

CHAPTER EIGHTEEN

"I am not mollified by your assurances," Billy Conroy said to Mickey Huntley. "My daughter will not survive in a federal prison. If I have to arrest her myself to guarantee her safety you can best believe that is what I'll do."

"You'll do nothing of the sort, daddy," Stella Conroy said to her father.

"Watch me," Billy said.

"This is terrible," interjected Brook Malanga. "I won't be the person who brings this sort of dissension to people I consider at least colleagues and at best friends. I'm revoking my hiring of you two right now."

"There's a way to proceed with this without jeopardizing anyone's freedom," Cooper Grey said quietly. "But it does require trust and bipartisanship."

"This isn't politics, Coop," I said grumpily.

"In its own small way yes it is, Cash." he said to me. "You and Stella parse information to Jeff and me that often doesn't include the full picture of just what you're doing."

"Of course we do," Stella said emphatically. She was clearly angry at her father and frustrated by the entire unfolding event. "You don't work for or with us. Why should you be included in how we decide to exercise our business decisions?"

"Because from time to time we are," Coop said evenly. "I ask you to remember the kidnapping of Mallory Weather."

"Agreed," I said. "That was a case where we needed your help. This is a case where we'd be putting you at significant risk by involving you."

"This time we can do what you can't," Coop said. "I worked for twenty years in the bail bond business. My license is still active. I can do things you can't. One time, you even saved my life, Cash. Isn't it time I repaid the favor?"

"Are you suggesting we let you take over this case?" I sounded incredulous. "Jeff isn't licensed. He'd be in immediate danger."

"Nobody bothers with two oystermen asking a few questions," Jefferson Davis said. I looked at him. He was having difficulty keeping a big grin from appearing on his handsome face.

At that moment, Sarah appeared. She'd been working in her inner sanctum. "Agent Beatrice Bush emailed a man I assume is her immediate superior, Roland Bishop, around five fifteen today. It seems there's been a disaster in the CIA's search for Eric Malanga."

Minerva chose that moment to rush from the laundry room to the front of the house chasing a huge but terrified water bug. Her yowls cut the atmosphere like a knife, and the cacophony was jarring. She killed and dissected the bug in the kitchen. For the first time in my life I could relate to the bug.

"Sarah?" Mickey finally said.

"Two deputies from Pender County murdered an active duty

marine they believed to be Eric Malanga this afternoon, outside of Rocky Point. The CIA is understandably distressed by this unfortunate turn of events and scrambling for some decent way to explain it. As an aside, I am tempted to say there is no good or decent way to explain it at all. He was a decorated marine with a wife and four children. There is, as yet, no official announcement of this tragedy. I suspect the CIA has ordered an information blackout until they have decided on a message. And there may never be a real message."

"My god," Brook Malanga exclaimed. "This is a nightmare. An innocent man is dead; my brother is an active target. This is too much. I don't know what to do or how to deal with this."

"We probably do," I said to Brook Malanga. Then I turned to Billy Conroy. "Get out of our way, Billy," I said evenly to him. "We have what and who we need to see this through."

The Sheriff looked at me. Then he looked at his daughter. "Stella?" he said.

"You heard my partner, daddy. If y'all won't help us just get out of the way."

"Your father's going to help you, Stella," Louise Dickson said to her. "Aren't you, Billy?"

Sheriff Billy Conroy sat down on the sofa in the great room of the house on Beach House Lane and took his hat off. He looked more tired than I have ever seen him.

"Yes," he said. "I'll help while repeating my reservations. Federal agencies do not believe in leeway unless you're well connected. But you two have gone this far and you've got to see your way through this one way or another. Still, if Jefferson is going to be involved, he needs to be deputized as well. Be at my office at eight o'clock tomorrow morning, son, and we'll see to it."

"Keep in mind their case is mightily compromised, Billy," Sarah Ehrenson said. "Their manhunt has resulted in the murder of an innocent; and a marine no less. Nobody is better at leveraging this kind of information than Mickey is."

"As usual," Mickey Huntley said with a smile, "Sarah is right."

CHAPTER NINETEEN

Sheriff Haskell Shorter was very uncomfortable. He was also sweating right through his uniform and in spite of his air conditioned office. Sitting across from him at his desk were Special Agent Beatrice Bush and one of her top lieutenants, Bart Clarkson. Neither was smiling.

"It's difficult for me to believe that we gave you instructions to issue a BOLO on the target, sheriff," Beatrice Bush said.

"It's automatic, ma'am," the sheriff said quietly.

"It hasn't been automatic in any of the other counties we visited today," she said. "Just yours; just in Pender County."

"We bend over backwards to cooperate with the federal law enforcement agencies, ma'am. It's in our blood. We're home to Lejeune."

"And now there's a dead marine's blood all over this department," she said. "This will not go unanswered. Where are the two deputies responsible for this?"

"I sent them home," the Sheriff said. "They're as close to a state of shock as I've ever seen them. Both are good men."

"And clearly overzealous," Bart Clarkson said. "The body has six bullet holes."

"We train them to shoot to kill when they feel their lives are in danger," Sheriff Haskell Shorter said. He could feel the sweat running down his back. "The man was reaching inside his jacket pocket."

"I'm aware of the cause, sheriff," Beatrice Bush said dismissively. "It's the effect that I'm now forced to deal with. I want both men's guns and shields on your desk within the hour."

"But I already told them I would assign them desk duty pending an investigation," the sheriff said.

"I have zero interest in what you told them," she said. "They are, as of this moment, dismissed from duty. I would point out that you yourself should be as well."

Sheriff Haskell Shorter felt his blood rising in his face. Before he could stop himself, he stood up, leaned his hands against his desk, and exclaimed, "Just a goddamned minute, you bitch; this county is sacred to me and my men. I won't have you destroying them and it because your twat's in a knot."

Bart Clarkson quickly rose to his feet but Beatrice Bush put her hand on his arm, shook her head and eased him back down on his chair. She was sanguine in her last response to the Pender County sheriff.

"I don't give a damn how you characterize me, sheriff. You are, after all, a product of your environment. But those two yahoos are done in law enforcement and you may well be, too. The Agency is now monitoring your office. The agent I have assigned is on his way and will need a desk and whatever else he requires. I will deal with the dead man's family. You will refrain from making any statement at all. Do we understand each other?"

Around eight o'clock in the morning on the day after Cassandra Quick overheard the conversation that changed her view of certain events, she and Cudworth Sweat were hauling an eighteen-foot aluminum skiff with a five horsepower Evinrude motor from her niece's house in Ivanhoe, North Carolina to the side of the Black River that bordered the small town itself.

"I know right where I launched it that day," she said to Cuddy. Fifteen minutes later, they were trolling upstream to where she'd met the man she recognized as Eric Malanga. "Right about here," Cassandra said and turned off the little motor.

"Did you leave before he did," Cuddy asked.

"No. That's why I know he went upstream. But once he hit that sharp curve up away I lost sight of him. I don't guess we'll be seeing much by way of landmarks to his camp but we'll see something." Cassandra turned the motor back on and they slowly meandered upstream. It was a beautiful day full of soft sunshine, myriad shades of green from the dense foliage that thrived by the river—and the river itself was nearly placid. As they rounded the curve where Eric Malanga had disappeared from sight that day, Cassandra's senses heightened. Cuddy was sitting in front of her, looking through a pair of binoculars.

"Watch for anything that looks like a ground disturbance, she said. "It may be a clearing and he'd need at least a small one. My guess is he'd choose the side away from town. It'd be safer, especially since he'd be dependent on fire."

The skiff kept up a decent clip for the next half hour without incident. They'd passed and waved at several other fishermen in their boats when Cuddy said forcefully, "Stop."

"Let me see," Cassandra said.

When her cousin handed her the binoculars and she took a look she studied what appeared to be a small clearing. She also noticed what she thought might be a garden patch. This could be wild, she knew, but when she saw corn husks, she wondered.

"For sure," she said. "We need to look at it right up close. It's a fair ways in."

"Few hundred feet is all," said Cuddy.

"But if nobody's looking," she started.

"Yes," he said. "They'd never notice it."

When they're secured the skiff they sat on the shore to talk. "If he's there, we're just exploring," Cassandra said. "He won't hurt us."

"You're certain," Cuddy said.

"Totally," she answered.

Fifty feet in, Cassandra put her hand on Cuddy's arm. They both stopped because they both heard voices.

"This ain't livable," a man said. "This here is old, most likely abandoned. We gotta call Homer, tell him false alarm. Most likely he be pissed but there it is. Ain't nothing for it."

"Let's get the hell out of here," another man with a high pitched voice said. "I'm city through and through. Anything country makes me greatly nervous."

"Car ain't but a half mile away; we book we're there in ten. Somethin' else maybe materialize tomorrow."

Then, after several minutes of silence, Cassandra Quick turned to her cousin. "Those were black men. Who in the world were they looking for; and if it's Eric Malanga, why?"

Minutes later, Cuddy kicked at the remains of a small campfire. "Smell it," Cassandra said.

"It's not new but it is recent," he answered. "Maybe this is his camp."

His cousin was looking around. "I know I saw some corn husks," she said, walking a bit further in. Twenty feet and sharply to the left, quite well-hidden behind a small copse of evergreens, brought her to a cultivated small square where there had been a pea patch, a scattering of tomatoes and potatoes, and a few stalks of corn. Adjacent to the small garden she noticed blueberry bushes and they were abundant. "Man could live quite easily here," Cassandra said. "At least until December. The cold would force him to seek shelter. And I wonder where he hides his rowboat? It'll be somewhere near here. He probably hides it in all this wild foliage."

When she noticed what she intuited was something buried, she called to Cuddy. "Over here, cousin. Grab something to dig with."

Cuddy handed her a large flat stone and kept one himself. In a few minutes they'd unearthed a metal box. Inside they saw a lot of change, some tens and twenties, official looking papers, and a few photographs. Cassandra scanned the paperwork.

"Yes," she said. "We found his camp. These are enlistment papers and official greetings. But it's the photographs that tell the story. This is the reason for his sorrow Cuddy," she said as she handed him a photo of a delicately beautiful Eurasian woman. In another, she and Eric were beaming into the camera, smiling happily, and holding hands. "They are obviously in love. Whatever happened to her is driving Eric Malanga to finish this journey he's on. And if I had to guess, I'd say she's dead."

"The postcard was the only clue," I said. "And Brooke received it two days before the CIA contacted her. All it said was 'Remember Ivanhoe.' Their family often spent time in that small community picking wild blueberries and fishing when both children were young. In the intervening years Brooke had forgotten all about it. But Eric hadn't. Both Stella and I believe he is there, somewhere, off the radar. It's beginning to mimic the needle in a haystack scenario. Even two leads we got from a reliable source yielded nothing." I sounded incredibly disgruntled and I was.

"Something bothering you," Cooper Grey asked.

"You're damned right there is," I answered dyspeptically. "I am bone tired of outside interference in my life and my work when I am not the one requesting it. And I resent the hell out of having to sit here today and have this discussion with you and Jefferson." I looked at the clock on the wall. "How long before he gets here," I said. "I don't want to talk about this twice."

"Cash," Coop began. But I'd had it.

"Oh just shut up, Cooper," I answered. "I know you're good at what you do. But Jeff has no business being included. He's no detective; he has zero experience in investigations. He's here because we're involved; nothing more."

Cooper ignored my anger. "I called a guy in the CIA this morning. I've known him for years. I didn't have to make up much of a story. I told him what I was doing; we swapped a few friendly words and then I asked what in hell the agency was doing all over southeastern North Carolina—looking for terrorists? The pause started to drag on longer than it should; finally he dropped his voice and said he couldn't talk about it but how did I know. I said everybody with good eyes and ears knew. His response was one word: Jesus! He quickly said he had a meeting to get to, so we said goodbye and he was gone. All Jeff and I will do is drive up to Ivanhoe and look around. It'll save you and Stella time and it might save lives."

"Well then, I should put you on the payroll," I said sarcastically.

"Do it if you want to, Cash. I know how good you are, too. It'd be an honor to work for you. For god's sake woman, you saved my life. And if I recall correctly, didn't Jefferson work for Stella at one time?"

"Are you trying to make me feel worse, Cooper Grey? All these work-related compliments and concessions are starting to feel phony."

Coop laughed. "That's because men generally don't give them," he said. "But consider for a minute who I'm married to, add in that what I say about my feelings for you is genuine, and let's get on with the work. And if you're ever inclined, you could learn to take a compliment."

As I was framing a response to him, Stella and Jeff walked in the door. Coop stood up, gave me a quick salute, grabbed Jeff by the elbow and said, "We've got our marching orders for the day, old son. Let's take my car. I feel like driving." As they were walking out the door, he turned and said, "I'll keep you informed, boss."

"What the fuck was that all about," Stella said to me.

I looked at her. "I think I just put those two on payroll," I said. "I'm starved. Let's hit on the Gulfstream for a good old-fashioned breakfast.

"Fine with me," my partner said. "But how the hell much are they going to cost us?"

"In the scheme of things," I said, "nothing."

"That works, I reckon."

CHAPTER TWENTY

Eric Malanga had visited most of the bars outside Camp Lejeune without luck, and his feet were tired when he walked into the Driftwood. The establishment was so close to the camp itself, he could see into it clearly. It was five o'clock in the afternoon but the place was nearly empty. A few people were shooting pool and a scattering of drinkers sat at the bar nursing beers or mixed drinks. He took a seat at the end of the bar closest to the front door, rested his feet on the lowest rung of the bar stool, and willed himself to relax. No one paid him the least bit of attention. After a couple of minutes, the bartender, who had been in deep conversation with a female patron at the other end of the slats, looked up and glanced around. When he noticed Eric, he nodded his head and walked over.

"Help you?" he said.

"Draft would be welcome," Eric said and smiled. "Bud's fine." As the bartender drew the draft, Eric took a hand full of peanuts from a bowl in front of him and suddenly realized how long it had been since he'd done such a simple thing as reach for a snack or wait for a draft beer. The peanuts were delicious. His first sip of the icy cold beer hit him immediately. He hadn't had a taste of any alcohol since the trouble in Burma broke. I'd better load up on these peanuts, he thought to himself. Then he noticed a small stack of menus leaning up against the wall to his left. He reached for one and opened it. When the bartender saw this he approached Eric.

"Like to order something?"

"You bet. A couple of double cheeseburgers will do it."

"Fries and slaw come with each of those."

"Great." Eric said.

In ten minutes, his order was in front of him along with bottles of ketchup and mustard and salt and pepper shakers. Twenty minutes later Eric was so pleasantly full and content, he thought he could easily fall asleep right here on this barstool.

As the bartender was removing the plates and laying the bill down next to his half-full glass of beer Eric said, "This place always so empty on a Friday afternoon?"

"You kidding? Normally it's so crowded you'd have waited an hour for that order."

"What's different about today?"

"Alls I know is what I've heard."

"Which is…?" Eric asked.

"Lejeune's on lockdown."

"Lockdown? Huh. I wonder why that happened."

"There's a homegrown terrorist threat is what a retired marine told me a while ago. Some guy went AWOL and is somewhere around here killing fellow marines. Some kind of grudge or mental disease or who the hell knows what all. Maybe just because the sun comes up in the morning. PTSD ain't no joke."

Eric Malanga never moved a facial muscle. Instead, he picked up the bill, paid it, left a tip and said, "Well, I hope the situation improves."

As he was walking out the door, the bartender said, "Oh, it will. They'll catch the poor son of a bitch eventually. Probably shoot his sorry ass to hell and back."

Once outside, Eric Malanga considered what he'd just heard and then considered his options. Almost immediately, he headed for his small shelter on the beach to pack up and head back to the relative safety of Ivanhoe. His plans had to change.

Maurice Big Daddy Washington looked at Homer. "His name is Eric Malanga?"

"Straight from New Hanover's source, boss. I had to lay out five bills to get it. This one's wrapped tighter than a dumb ass mummy. And the two boys I sent to scout around for this dude came up empty. Twice."

Big Daddy nodded. "See Moses on your way out of the store, Homer. He'll reimburse the expense. And don't forget to sign the receipt."

"Am I done?"

"For now. Keep your ears to the ground and your eyes on the prize. Call me with anything."

"Always, boss. I hear, you hear," Homer said on his way out of the room.

Once he was alone, Big Daddy googled Eric Malanga. To his astonishment, he got nothing at all. After thirty minutes of searching he was forced to conclude that whoever this man was, his identity had been completely wiped off the face of the earth. There was no Eric Malanga, at least on paper. As with most things in Maurice Washington's world, the information he wanted out of this situation was simply to provide him knowledge that he might use as leverage, should he ever be faced with federal charges due to his drug-related activities.

He was aware of the interest the FBI had in busting him and charging him with enough felonies to guarantee that he'd spend the rest of his life in a federal prison. This CIA mess with the elusive Eric Malanga might well provide him with that leverage. He knew it was a cluster fuck.

As he was winding up his store business and looking forward to dinner out with his wife, it dawned on Big Daddy that perhaps he already had the information he needed. There had been no official or unofficial reports at all about the death of an active duty marine at the hands of two Pender County Sheriff's deputies who mistook him for Malanga, and there likely never would be.

There was a total blackout surrounding the entire unfortunate incident. It was a cover-up engineered by the Feds and obeyed by the locals, and although he didn't know exactly why the Agency wanted Eric Malanga dead, he didn't need to know. Direct knowledge of the cover-up itself was as good as gold. Tomorrow he'd write down what he knew, file it in his safety deposit box, and worry less about the danger the FBI posed to his business. Not a bad few days' work he thought to himself as he considered what he was going to order for dinner. Maurice Big Daddy Washington was whistling happily as he drove his latest restored classic Chrysler Continental with suicide doors to his waterfront home in Wrightsville Beach.

Sheriff Billy Conroy drove past the designated parking area for visitors to Sargasso Vineyards and finally stopped just outside the door of the huge barn where wine was produced and juice was bottled. There was a hum of activity inside the building. When he exited his car and entered the structure, the first person he saw was Junior Fisk and one other man busily working over a huge box of grapes.

"Y'all know where I might could find Paul Sargasso," he said to Junior.

Junior stopped what he was doing and looked at the Sheriff. "Last time I seen him he was fiddling with those cabernet grapes of his," Junior said. "Walk straight back through there you'll run smack into him."

A few minutes later, he was face to face with Sargasso. "Afternoon," he said to the man.

"Sheriff Conroy," Sargasso said, clearly startled to see him. "Is there news?"

"Y'all got somewhere we can speak more privately," Billy said.

"Not really unless we go to my house which is a fair distance from here. I have no objection to talking now. This amount of privacy is okay with me."

"That's fine. Well, from what I can figure, Mr. Sargasso, your trouble is directly related to your brother's production and distribution of as yet unregulated mind-altering drugs. My calculation is that someone's child has been damaged or died as a result of ingesting them. It's not likely to stop without you rein in your brother's dangerous activities or frankly speaking even if you do, considerin' the damage has probably already been done. Y'all need to be aware of the fact that I will be notifying the DEA regarding this situation. You'll want to be prepared to tell them whatever they decide to ask both you and your brother, and anyone else involved in this situation. It may take quite a while to find out who the actual perpetrator of your own property damages is, but they'll find that person or persons eventually. Once I hand it over to the Feds it's entirely within their jurisdiction and I'm officially done."

Paul Sargasso stared at Billy Conroy. His face suddenly drained of color and then his knees buckled. He just collapsed and sat down hard on the concrete floor of the barn. He opened his mouth as though he was about to speak, but nothing came out. Billy Conroy bent his knees so he could look at the man eye to eye.

"Are you all right?" he asked.

Again, Paul Sargasso opened his mouth. What came out was a sort of choking sound. Finally, after a series of harsh coughs, he said simply "How do you know anything about my brother?" His voice sounded like loose gravel.

Billy smiled at him. "Let's get you back on your feet, Mr. Sargasso." He practically lifted Paul Sargasso back up to a standing position and leaned him against the back wall of the barn for a bit of support. A minute later, Paul Sargasso looked at him beseechingly.

"I don't know anything about my brother's business except that he assures me that his activities are not illegal. And his work is entirely unrelated to my vineyard business. He is my winemaker and then he has, as you now know, his own interests. He's a gifted chemist."

"Well, that's the kind of information you'll want to give to the DEA once they begin their investigation. I need to caution y'all not to try to erase your brother's activities ahead of the Feds because I have a set of pictures of his activities, including his set of books. While it's true that what he is doing may not be against the law, that is most likely due to the fact that he has remained under the radar. That can change in an instant once someone is damaged physically or mentally because of ingesting his product. Y'all clear on that point?"

"Yes, yes, of course," Paul Sargasso said. "How long before they begin?"

"No idea," Billy Conroy said. "Could be a day, could be a week, could be a year. Depends on how busy they are. But I suspect they'll be in touch sooner rather than later."

"Will you tell me how you found out about my brother," Paul Sargasso said again.

"Mr. Sargasso, that information really shouldn't concern you. There are some things in law enforcement that are controlled by what I call a need to know. In this instance, you really have no need to know. If there's something that comes up that I should hear about, like more damage to your property, y'all know where to find me." Sheriff Billy Conroy tipped his hat, turned and walked back to the front door. He passed Junior Fisk and the other man still working on the box of grapes, winked quickly at Junior, got to his car and drove away.

CHAPTER TWENTY ONE

The lockdown of Camp Lejeune had been ordered by the commanding Brigadier General of the camp shortly after his hastily arranged meeting with CIA Special Agent Beatrice Bush and Agent Bart Clarkson. He had been told a blatant lie to convince him to order the lockdown. It was a lie that would be repeated so many times that it would forever be seen as the truth by most people: a rogue agent had escaped a federal jurisdiction to seek revenge on the CIA itself and on the branch of the military that the escapee had served in; namely, the marines. Beatrice Bush had told it as easily as she drew breath.

By the following morning, when Eric Malanga was about to begin his search for Clay Carpenter, every marine at Camp Lejeune had a copy of the photo of him that CIA agents were passing out to Post Offices all over southeastern North Carolina and northeastern South Carolina. The Brigadier General had also been assured that the dead marine who had served under his command had died a hero even though he had been tragically outgunned by the rogue agent. He would receive a hero's funeral and a twenty-four-gun salute. His family would be taken care of monetarily, and would even be allowed to remain in free housing on the base until all of the children reached eighteen years of age, if the widow so wished.

Security at all gates had been enhanced and marines were now inspecting every arriving vehicle, much like is done at the border of Mexico and America. They did not want this killer arriving hidden in a trunk or a back seat or underneath a vehicle.

For his part, on his way back to Ivanhoe Eric Malanga never took a main or secondary road. He walked all through the night over fields and off-road vehicle tracks, under a nearly full moon and steered by the stars. Less than twenty four hours after he had packed up his gear on a beach in Jacksonville, North Carolina, he was standing next to the small boat he kept behind a deserted shack with a caved-in roof on the opposite shore from his camp on the Black River.

It was three thirty in the afternoon and the day was filled with warm sunshine and song birds and active jumping river fish. When he'd rowed the skiff across the river he exited it; then he pulled it up and out of the water and hauled it fifty feet downstream from his garden patch and stored it hidden behind a fallen log. Then he sat down on the log to rest. A few hours earlier and unbeknownst to him he had had visitors. Cassandra Quick and Cudworth Sweat were now aware of where to find him. It was merely a question of when and with whom they would visit him again.

"They've locked down Camp Lejeune," Sarah said to Stella and me. "The order was issued last night by the commanding brigadier general. You'd better go on the assumption that he's been sold a huge bag of goods, until I can confirm it one way or another. The fact that no statements have hit the media about the death of that active duty marine tells me that the CIA has decided on one hell of a cover up. And if Eric Malanga is unaware of this he may be about to walk right into a trap. He'd probably be dead before he hit the ground."

"Until we locate him there's nothing we can do," I said. The three of us were sitting outside the cottage in short shorts and halters getting a little sun. When Stella's phone rang it startled all of us.

"Stella Conroy," my partner said, holding the phone flat in her hand.

"This is Cassandra Quick," the voice on the other end of the line said. "Do you remember me?"

"Not right off. Remind me," Stella said.

"That murder case a few years ago where an Indian was charged," Cassandra said. "You proved him innocent."

"The Lumbee case," Stella said. "Sure. Y'all made me an honorary member of your tribe. I took that as a real high honor. Are you the woman who gave me the meditation chants?"

"I am," said Cassandra Quick. "And now I'm about to give you an even bigger gift. But you aren't in your office. Are you somewhere nearby? I'm parked at your building right now."

"I'm not more than five minutes away," Stella said. "I'm sitting in front of a cottage on Beach House Lane. That's a small…"

"I know where it is," Cassandra said. "I'll see you in a few minutes. Y'all might want your partner there, too."

"She's sitting right next to me," said Stella.

"Good," Cassandra said as she ended the call.

"Any idea what that was all about?" I asked.

"Not one clue. These Lumbee people are kinda sorta strange. If I remember correctly, this woman is a bit psychic." Stella shrugged. "We'll find out."

Anthony Sargasso listened patiently to his brother, noting the level of anxiety in his voice, and when Paul stopped speaking, he said calmly "We're not without resources, Paul. I'll call my attorney right away. This will sort itself out."

"It's the DEA for Christ's sake," Paul Sargasso said heatedly. "I don't want them swarming all over my property while they sort. I run a winery. The public is welcome."

"And the profit made from chemistry has given you the time to make it viable," Anthony said. "Believe me, I don't want interference from the federal government any more than you do. Whatever my attorney advises is what I'll do. But we both need to speak with him as quickly as possible."

"That Sheriff would not tell me how he even knew about your work, Tony. I keep thinking about that and it's driving me crazy."

Anthony Sargasso thought about that for a half a minute before he said, "What difference does it make? He knows. This is low country in a backwards crazy southern state. For all we know, there are sources all over on law enforcement books looking to make a buck. And nothing about what I do is secret. It's in plain sight if somebody decides to look. And somebody did."

Agent Bart Clarkson and his boss, Special Agent Beatrice Bush, drove into Ivanhoe at two o'clock in the afternoon on the day after Clarkson had been scheduled to visit it. They parked in front of the post office and entered the small structure. Five people were waiting in line for one thing or another. Several more were at standing at counters addressing packages to be mailed.

"Let's get a coffee, Bea." Bart said. "This'll clear out in fifteen minutes or so."

"Get a coffee where," she asked. "This is nothing but a half-horse town."

"Gotta be somewhere," he said. "Won't hurt to look."

There were four men sitting at a table outside a doctor's office across the street and down from the post office. Two were white. Two were black. One of the white men noticed the two CIA agents. "Go get the car," he said evenly to the other white man, reaching in his pants pocket and handing him the keys. "Don't hurry. Don't turn around, just go." Then he smiled at the two black men. "This is an old picture," he said. "By now this man may be dark enough to pass. He's been living outside for a year or more. Have you noticed a new blueberry picker or a new hog man? Look at the features not the color."

"It seem like maybe…" one of the black men said. "We had a newbie pickin' berries last month. He didn't stay. Collected two weeks wages and left."

"And he resembled this man?"

"He was more muscled. Thinner. Real long hair. A nice fella but real quiet like he got a load on his mind he can't shake."

"Did he ever say where he lived?"

"I ain't wanna put this man in a cross hair," the other black man said. "He was a good guy."

"You won't," Cooper Grey said. "I'm trying to find him to help him."

"Well, the only thing he said was he lived off the river. That rung true. So do I."

When Jefferson Davis pulled the Altima to the curb, Cooper Grey stood up, slipped a pair of sunglasses on, shook each man's hand, dropped fifty dollars on the table and said simply, "You've been incredibly helpful, gentlemen. Thank you."

As they were driving out of Ivanhoe, Coop turned to look at Jefferson. "Reason we're leaving? The CIA guy who interviewed us early last week is parked in front of the post office. There's a woman with him. It looks like they may be about to find out that Stella and Cash are also trying to locate Eric Malanga."

"Y'all better call Mickey's office. If she's not there Darius will be able to find her to tell her to meet us back at the cottage. Tell him to give us an hour to get there ourselves."

———————————————

Stella and I had put shirts on over our halters and we were walking back outside when Cassandra Quick pulled into one of the designated parking spots on the ocean front side of the cottage. A man was sitting next to her.

After making introductions all around—Cassandra Quick had introduced the man as her cousin, Cuddy—Sarah suggested we all move inside where we would be more comfortable. Our guests chose two side-by-side wicker chairs. Stella sat on one of the sofas and I perched on a bar stool beside the kitchen counter. Sarah, as is her wont whenever we have guests, repaired to the kitchen.

"Would anyone like something cold to drink," she asked as she opened the refrigerator door. "Or a snack? I have brie cheese and cracked pepper biscuits and a jar of Greek olives. Beer would be lovely with that. Or wine."

"That sounds good, Sarah," Stella said. "Beer's good with me." Everybody nodded.

"It's good to see you, Cassandra," Stella said to the woman. "How long has it been?"

Cassandra Quick glanced at her hands before she said, "Four years this November. And today I have got a long and winding story to relate and I may wander off a straight path while I tell it but it's imperative that I begin. A man's life is at stake."

CHAPTER TWENTY TWO

Mickey Huntley was in court when Cooper Grey called her office. "Mickey Huntley's office," Darius Millar said. "May I help you?"

"Is she around?" Cooper answered.

"She's always around, Coop," Darius said blithely. "At the moment she's in court on a divorce case. Why?"

"Any idea when she'll be finished?"

"She blocked off two hours which was up fifteen minutes ago. Y'all got some kind of emergency?"

"I'd say yes but I don't know whether she'd agree with me or not."

"Tell me what you want her to know," Darius said. "I'll text her."

"The feds are in Ivanhoe."

"That's it?"

"Yep."

"Okay. She's informed. Where are you in case I need to reach you?"

"Jeff and I are on the road headed back to the cottage in Carolina Beach. We sure hope that Mickey can join us. We're about forty minutes out."

At that moment, a text arrived on Darius's phone. "Give me a second, Coop. I just got a message." Moments later, he said, "She says she'll be done in ten and on her way to the cottage. Is that enough?"

"Perfect."

Special Agent Beatrice Bush looked at the Ivanhoe postmaster and thought he might just be one hundred years old. She could not decide whether his memory was agile or atrophied.

"You're certain this is the same picture you saw a few days ago?" she said skeptically.

"Yes ma'am," the happy little man responded.

"From two women you'd never seen before?"

"And both damned good looking women they were too. Very pleasant on the eyes and very polite."

The fucking South is obsessed with politeness which is the farce of the ages when you consider how they treat women as chattel and Black Americans as trash, Bea Bush thought to herself. Out loud she said, "Did they say why they were looking for him?"

"One said a sister was looking for her brother," the postmaster answered. "I told them and I'm telling you the man in this photograph does not live in Ivanhoe. I am total positive on that."

"Bea," Bart Clarkson said quietly. "It's gotta be those two who found the corpse. I could not have been more adamant they were to remain hands off."

"Corpse!" the postmaster said loudly. "What corpse?" A woman who had just entered the post office as he uttered those words dropped the bunch of letters she was carrying in her hand and stared at the three of them.

Beatrice Bush realized she was grinding her teeth and forced herself to stop. "My colleague misspoke," she said to the agitated man behind the counter. Clarkson had moved to pick up the letters that had scattered all over the floor. "This inquiry has nothing to do with a deceased person." Although the postmaster looked unconvinced, he nodded his head.

As they turned to leave the building, she said to the postmaster, "Thank you for your cooperation. We'll note that the man we're looking for doesn't live in Ivanhoe. Have a nice day."

When they were resettled in their car, Beatrice Bush said very quietly and evenly, "Get me the hell out of this god forsaken backwater swamp and into civilization. I have had about all I can take of the North Carolina populace and countryside. And I'm staring at a disaster in the making. If we don't find Eric Malanga soon, I am going to be manning an office in Shitscreek, South Dakota, where the crime of the century is shoplifting."

———————————

"One afternoon in Spring I was fishing out of my niece's skiff on the Black River in Ivanhoe," Cassandra Quick said. "During the course of the day I encountered another fisherman and we exchanged pleasantries. He was a soft-spoken man and what was clear to me, although he didn't remark on them, was his troubles. Now it's important that y'all keep in mind I have a memory like a photograph. Once you hit my eyes, I record you. If I see you again, I remember you. Maybe I don't place you right off, but eventually I do."

I looked at Stella. Her mouth was open slightly as though she was about to speak but she didn't. Sarah was sitting beside me and inexplicably put her hand on my knee. I glanced at her but she was looking intently at Cassandra Quick.

"Last week I was at my post office box in Pembroke, when I noticed two official-looking men talking to our postmaster. They left and I asked him what the conversation was about. He showed me a photograph of a man in uniform and said the Feds were looking for a murderer. When I looked at the picture I knew I'd seen him before. I was actually on my way to meet Cuddy about another unrelated matter, that I also need to talk with you about, when I remembered I'd met that man earlier in spring when we were both fishing on the Black River. I tell you without hesitation that this man is not a murderer. But the CIA is indeed looking for him and yesterday afternoon Cuddy and I found him. Well, we found his camp. He's likely to return to it. In fact, he may be there now. His name is Eric Malanga. I believe you are also looking for him. If we leave today we can reach his camp in two or three hours. I'm not certain there is a lot of time to waste."

"Jesus Christ," Sarah mumbled to the room at large.

"Y'all found him?" I don't think I've ever heard Stella sound so incredulous. "I mean his camp?"

"We did," Cuddy said. "And when we walked ashore a couple of black men had also found the camp but didn't know what it was. They thought it was an abandoned site. Cassandra and I can't even speculate on why they'd even be looking. But they left without spotting us."

I looked at Stella. "Big Daddy, probably," I said.

"Most likely," she said. "But why?"

"An addiction to information," I answered. "He never knows what'll prove to be important. But he's not a player in this. I'd discount those two men as incidental except to him."

"Well, Cassandra's right about one thing," Stella said. "We do not have a lot of time to waste. We'd best return to Ivanhoe this afternoon. If we leave now, there'll be a window of daylight left when we hit the river."

We were changing into more appropriate garb—blue jeans, sweatshirts, and running shoes—when we heard a car pull into one of the parking spaces beside the cottage. Then we heard two doors open and slam shut. A minute later, Cooper Grey said, "Anybody home?" Stella, who was dressed in a pair of my jeans and one of Sarah's Georgetown sweatshirts, left my bedroom and walked to the living room.

"We're gettin' ready to drive to Ivanhoe," she said to Coop and Jefferson. "We know where Eric Malanga is."

"So do we," Jeff said. "He's most likely got a camp beside the Black River. But the reason we're here is to get you out of the way for a while. The feds hit Ivanhoe earlier today so by now they know you two were looking for Malanga."

"We do not have time to 'get out of the way' right now," I said, walking up to stand next to Stella. Cassandra Quick and her cousin had been sitting quietly on the far side of the living room.

I don't think either of the boys even noticed them until Cassandra said, "We can go to Ivanhoe and not be seen. My niece's house is out of the way. The cops would never spot you there. And we don't need daylight to find his camp. All we need is a couple flashlights for when the moon won't do. But it's nearly full right now. And tonight'll be clear. The moon will probably do just fine without any help from us."

"Who's this?" Coop said.

"An old friend of mine," Stella said. "Cassandra Quick and her cousin Cuddy meet my husband Cooper Grey and his friend Jeff Davis."

Sarah joined us, wearing black cargo pants and a purple sweatshirt.

"And it's a long story" she said, "which we can relate as we drive back to Ivanhoe. I suggest we all pile into the big Mercedes. The feds never pegged it so we won't be stopped. Oh, here comes Mickey. Well, there's room for eight of us if we're careful."

"That's not the best way to play this, Sarah," I said. "Stella will drive her car to her home. We'll follow and pick her up there. The boys can drive the car they came in. Cassandra and her cousin can do likewise. We all have GPS. Once Cassandra gives us her relative's address in Ivanhoe we can each find our way there. Oh, and Mickey can leave her car in that parking lot next to the community gym. We'll pick her up after we get Stella."

So that's what we did and by five fifteen that evening we all had landed back in Ivanhoe at a house we considered safe from prying eyes where a good-sized fishing boat was also ready and waiting.

CHAPTER TWENTY THREE

Beatrice Bush was pacing back and forth across the living room floor of her suite of rooms that overlooked the Cape Fear River at the Wilmington Hilton. She was also carrying her cell phone in her left hand because she was waiting to hear from an agent she had dispatched to an address in Carolina Beach, North Carolina.

"You want onions or olives, Bea?" Bart Clarkson asked her. He was mixing a batch of very dry gin martinis at the small but well-stocked bar in the far right corner of the room.

"Onions," she said perfunctorily. "You know I don't like green olives unless they're stuffed with almonds."

"I do know that," he said. "And there's an unopened jar of almond stuffed green olives sitting right here."

"Really," she said. "Imagine that…a ray of sunshine in all this gloom. Give me some of each, then; two or three olives, four or five onions. The way I feel at the moment I may be content to call that dinner."

"Not a chance," Clarkson said. "After a couple of these bruisers you'll want some real food. And you'll need some, too."

The loud ring of her cell phone interrupted their conversation.

"Yes," she said.

"It's Lenny, Boss. I'm at that Beach House Lane cottage but nobody else is. Delaney's Jaguar is parked in the adjacent lot. There aren't any other cars around. No lights on in the place. It's deserted, looks like."

"Who else lives there?" she asked. "Anyone?"

"Somebody named S. Ehrenson. Name's on the mailbox along with Delaney's."

"Hang on a second," Beatrice Bush said to her field agent. To Bart Clarkson she said, "Do we know someone named Ehrenson who lives with that Delaney woman?"

"Not that I'm aware of," he said. "Is it important?"

"Jesus, Bart." she snapped, "I don't know if it is or isn't but we need to find out one way or another. Get someone on it who can find out in a hurry. Go right to Langley. We don't have an unlimited window of time to work with here." To her field agent Lenny she said, "Are there neighbors around?"

"There are two or three cottages on Delaney's street. Lights are on. Do you want me to inquire?"

"Yes. Politely. Give it an air of importance that we need to contact Ms. Delaney ASAP about a legal matter involving her work as a private investigator and we really need their help. Don't mention the agency. Just flash your shield."

"Got it. I'll call as soon as I know anything boss."

Bart Clarkson had walked out of the living room onto the small terrace where two easy chairs were side by side. He sat down in one and set his drink on the little metal table beside it. Then he took his cell phone out of his jacket pocket, opened his contacts page, chose an entry, and hit a button. His call was answered after two rings.

"Fulton," said a female voice.

"This is Bart Clarkson calling for Beatrice Bush," he said. "I need information on someone as quickly as you can get it."

"Name?" she asked.

"Last name Ehrenson. First initial S."

"You do not know the gender?"

"No. My guess is female. An age approximation would be thirty five to forty. The address is Beach House Lane, Carolina Beach, NC 28428-4041."

"One moment."

Clarkson rested his Android on his lap and picked up his drink. He took a good swig from the martini, sighed, and ate two of his four olives. Then he took another satisfying swallow and put the drink back on the little table.

"I have a Sarah Ehrenson at that address," the woman named Fulton said. "She is 36 years old. She has a PhD from Georgetown University in political science. She works with a private investigative office run by a Katherine Delaney and a Stella Conroy where she is in charge of all pertinent research requests, which we often translate into data hacking, but that is not mentioned here so I note it only in passing. Anecdotally, she is a lesbian and she is in a long-term relationship with a defense attorney by the name of Mickey Huntley who is apparently highly regarded in the nearby city of Wilmington, North Carolina. Is this your person of interest?"

"Yes. I appreciate your help, Fulton. And thank you."

Clarkson ended the call, returned his cell phone to his jacket pocket and picked up his drink to finish it. As he was doing so, Beatrice Bush walked out to the small terrace carrying her empty glass and sat in the chair next to his.

"Anything?" she asked.

"Sarah Ehrenson shares the cottage on Beach House Lane with Delaney. Fulton, at Langley, tells me she's 36 years old, a PhD in Political Science from Georgetown and she makes her living as a computer analyst for a private investigative agency run by Delaney and Conroy. Fulton mentioned that computer analyst may also imply data hacker but that wasn't mentioned in our information file so she noted it only in passing. Bottom line is we have no way to assess what they do or do not know and no good way to find out short of finding them."

Beatrice Bush said nothing, but she handed her glass to Bart Clarkson who nodded, stood up, and went to fix another drink for both of them. As he started to pour, he heard her cell phone ring.

"Yes," she said.

"Lenny again, boss. The next door neighbor, a single guy, says a bunch of people all left the cottage in several different cars around three thirty-four o'clock this afternoon. He recognized most of them. Stella Conroy drove her Mustang herself and she left alone. Delaney rode with Ehrenson, who was driving a big Mercedes SUV. Delaney's boyfriend and Conroy's husband drove away together in a car he didn't recognize. And there was a lawyer that he thinks is Ehrenson's girlfriend who was driving an old red car he thought was a Nash and she was by herself. Finally, he saw two strangers, an impressive blond and a dark-skinned man, in a tan or grey Celica that he'd never seen before. That's it."

After thinking about what he'd related, Beatrice Bush said, "There are three other places in Carolina Beach I want you to check for signs of life. Conroy's house; she's on Charlotte Avenue. The boyfriend's boat, the Portofino, at the town pier, and the office itself on Lake Park Boulevard. Call me with anything you learn."

Bart Clarkson handed her a second drink. "Don't chug this one, Bea. Sip it. I just put an order in for two three-pound lobsters with sides of lyonnaise potatoes and roasted Brussels sprouts with bacon and honey butter."

If she was paying him the least bit of attention, she gave no sign of it. She half-drained her second drink, ate all of the stuffed olives which she chewed very carefully, and finally turned to him and said, "Apparently, Ms. Ehrenson is gay and her lover is a lawyer. Did we know that?"

"Yes," he said. "Fulton told me as much when I spoke with her; the lawyer is a woman by the name of Mickey Huntley. It didn't strike me as particularly relevant."

"We couldn't possibly know whether it's relevant or not until we know who this Mickey Huntley is, what kind of lawyer she is," Beatrice said to him. "Find out what you can, if anything, from Quantico."

Bart Clarkson nodded and stood to go back into the living room to make the call. He was halfway in when she said, "Wait. Don't bother with Quantico. I know a local FBI agent; give me a minute to think of his name." She drained her second drink, ate the five little pearl onions that remained, shook her head back and forth a few times and suddenly said, "Keating. Donald or David or Daniel. Something that starts with D. anyway. Call the local office. Someone is always there. If Keating isn't, get his home number or wherever he can now be reached. I don't care if it's Borneo. Find him."

Fifteen minutes later, two things happened. There was a rapid knocking on the door of the suite and Bart Clarkson announced to a still terrace-sitting Beatrice Bush that he had located Agent David Keating, who was in charge of the local branch of the FBI.

"He's on his way here as we speak, Bea. He doesn't want to talk over unsecured lines. He says it'll take him an hour and a half, two hours to arrive depending on traffic. He's in Fayetteville at the moment." As he finished this statement, he opened the door to the suite and a waiter walked in with their meal.

"This looks great," Bart Clarkson said. "And I'm starving." Beatrice Bush was about to sit down at the table when he reached for her chair and held it for her.

"You want a glass of chardonnay, Bea?" he asked.

"I want another martini. If Keating doesn't want to talk over an unsecured line when all we want is a bit of information about an active defense attorney in Wilmington, we are in for some troubling news, my friend."

Just how troubling it was remained something neither one of them could come close to fathoming until Agent David Keating finally arrived to explain.

CHAPTER TWENTY FOUR

Mickey Huntley, Stella and I rode with Sarah in the big Mercedes SUV for the trip back to Ivanhoe. Nobody did much talking and Sarah had the radio tuned to an oldies station. When Jefferson Airplane's startling Nineteen Sixties song hit the atmosphere, it seemed to rattle the windows in this tight and expensive automobile.

"When the truth is found to be lies; and all the joy within you dies. Don't you want somebody to love; don't you need somebody to love; wouldn't you love somebody to love. You better find somebody to love." Grace Slick was bouncing off all the walls. Her voice was shattering whatever was left of normal.

"Turn it down, Sarah, please," Mickey said. "We need to think out loud about something."

"I'll turn it off," Sarah replied. "It's not the sort of song you necessarily need to hear; especially now with the shape our country is in." The silence was stark. It almost left me feeling bereft; for what, I didn't know.

We were nearing the end of North College Road when Mickey said to Sarah, "Pull into the Best Buy which is coming up on your right. We need some throwaway phones. The CIA, if they're looking for us, can tap into any of our personal devices and we're not in the business of helping them succeed in finding us at the moment. In fact, we should all turn our phones off at this point. Otherwise, GPS can trace them.

"Mine has been off since this morning," I said.

"Mine hasn't been on for a few hours," Sarah said.

"I left mine at home," said my partner. Finally, Mickey shut hers off and put it in the big glove compartment of the Mercedes.

As Sarah pulled into the parking lot she said, "You can buy a couple of prepaids to be used in a dire emergency, Mickey; but remember, while the caller is untraceable the location isn't. We'd be much better off using my computer and Skype when we want to get in touch with someone. We're virtually untraceable by name and location, even if the person we call has an Automatic Identification Number."

"Prepaids are traceable to a specific location?" the lawyer asked.

"Not the specific address necessarily; but certainly a fairly precise location within the county. They'd know we were in Ivanhoe and that's more than we want them to know."

"OK. But I need at least one prepaid. I've got to call Brooke Malanga to let her know she needs to join us in Ivanhoe, and not only to be on hand when we locate her brother. If I know the Feds, they'll figure she's a player in this fairly quickly, and I don't want her at the mercy of the kind of interrogation they're very good at. I think they'd break her pretty easily and anyway it's nothing she deserves to be subjected to."

Sarah had parked the SUV in the first row of parking spots. "Be right back," Mickey said.

When Mickey returned to the car, she asked Sara to activate the prepaid. Then she dialed Brooke Malanga's office. When it was answered, she said, "Brooke. This is Mickey. Just listen. We are on our way to Ivanhoe. Your brother has been located. Leave your office now and drive to 4289 Ivanhoe Road. Your GPS will find it. We'll either be there or will be there shortly. If we're not there, tell the owner of the house you are a friend of her aunt Cassandra Quick and you'll be welcomed. Is this clear?"

"Yes. I'm leaving now."

"Good. And Brooke, turn off your cell phone. I'll explain when I meet you."

Ten minutes later, we had crossed Market Street and were now on the open highway that would deliver us to Ivanhoe in a little over an hour.

"I can't reach Stella," Sheriff Billy Conroy said to Louise Dickson. "I've been callin' her for over an hour. Her phone just goes to voicemail."

"Maybe she's turned it off. She may be taking a nap or she may be working where she has to turn it off. Are you saying you're worried?"

"I don't guess I know exactly what I am sayin'," he said with a frown. "But Stella don't normally turn off her phone when she's napping. She's always concerned when she does that she'll miss somethin' needs her attention right quick."

"Call Cash," Louise said. "She'll know where Stella is." She was pouring them each a cup of coffee, something she often did at the end of a workday. It gave them a reason to sit and enjoy the heady brew and chat about their various dealings and interactions with their community. It was her favorite part of the job.

"Damn it," Billy said heatedly. "I got more voicemail from

Delaney's phone. Something's goin' on, Louise. I feel it in my bones. Damn it to hell. Both those girls know how much I purely hate bein' kept in the dark."

Louise handed him his mug of coffee and put hers on the front of his desk as she sat in the more comfortable of the two visitor's chairs that faced him. Maybe he's right to be concerned, she thought to herself.

"Do you have Sarah Ehrenson's number," she said to him. "If you don't I do."

"No, I do not," he snapped.

"I'll get my phone, Billy. Try to relax. Take a nice sip of your coffee. We'll find them."

When she returned with her phone, she sat back down and dialed a number. Then she ended that call and dialed again. "Well," she said, "nobody's available. Sarah's goes to voicemail, too."

"They're up to no good," he said darkly. "They're closin' in on that AWOL marine worked for the CIA that those Feds thought was dead. I am scared for them, Louise. I am truly scared. Those Feds think that guy is a murderer and whether he is or not don't really matter to them. They say he is and they want him. Obstructing a federal investigation when you've been warned to stay away is certain jail time once they corner you. Or they could decide you're just nothin' but an obstacle standing in their way and shoot you dead, they get that chance. What in this world can I do? I love these women. None of them deserves to go to prison and Stella would not survive it. And it's for certain she or any one of them do not deserve to die."

"We've got to think, to strategize, Billy. Who can help us? Coop may know something or Jefferson. How about Mickey Huntley? Shall we see if we can locate any of them?" Louise Dickson was genuinely concerned for him. She had watched his eyes fill with tears he had quickly wiped away and it crossed her mind that she hadn't seen him cry in years. The last time was when his wife had died and he had been inconsolable for weeks.

"I do not have the emotional fortitude to just sit here and make phone calls, Louise. I've got to move, and I need your company. I'll be drivin' first to Stella's, then to Jeff's boat, then to Coop's condo, then to Mickey's office. If we strike out everywhere, I don't quite know what I'll do then. But I'll be doin' something. You game?"

"Always, Billy." she said. "Always."

Eric Malanga was worried. He was sitting on a blanket he'd placed next to a small fire he'd built on the far left side of his camp by the Black River and he was trying to decide if he should risk paying a visit to his sister Brooke or if such a move would put her at unnecessary and possibly physically dangerous risk. If he decided to do it, he'd have to leave pretty soon and he'd have to power walk from here to Topsail Beach. He thought he could make it in about 10 hours which would get him there while it was still dark if he left by eight. But if the CIA had decided to watch her house 24-7, they'd likely spot him even in the dark and all hell would break loose.

He hadn't been hungry for most of the day after he'd returned from that tavern outside Camp Lejeune but at the moment, which he figured was around five o'clock in the evening, he heard his stomach growl. Currently, his food supply was limited and it was too late to go fishing. He could make blueberry tea and toast his left over rolls on a stick. There was some beef jerky in his backpack and he could fry the potatoes that weren't yet rotten in his garden. He hoisted himself up and started collecting what he'd need for his supper.

Fifteen minutes later, he had four potatoes frying in an old iron skillet he'd found at the dump, three rolls ready to toast on a stick, blueberry tea steeping in a teapot he'd bought at the little grocery store he frequented, jerky warming on a board he often used for cooking his fish, and he'd also found a half dozen apples on an old apple tree at the back of his camp that he cherished. Most of those he'd place in his backpack if he decided to go to his sister's house. Two he'd eat tonight for his dessert. The size and content of this meal would give him the energy he needed to power walk to Topsail. That was one worry he could eliminate.

Eric Malanga knew he had other options. He knew he was an inconvenience the Agency didn't want to deal with. But he also knew that he could simply turn himself in to the CIA and hope for the best. He was also aware that receiving "the best" was unlikely to happen. What was likely was his "disappearance." They do not revel in having to explain their policy failures. And what was worse, he was already dead to them. They'd written him off a long time ago.

He also knew he really could just disappear. He could hitchhike to Montana or Idaho or South Dakota and simply evaporate into thin air. Or he could blend into a city like Seattle or Vancouver, Washington. If he chose to remain on the East Coast, the state of Maine offered multiple opportunities to live under the radar. And then there were the Florida Keys. He could fish for a living. He could build a lean-to himself. If he had to choose, his choice of locations was myriad: Little Torch Key appealed to him; so did Big Coppitt Key, Ramrod Key, and Sugarloaf Key.

He could also, of course, leave the country. This was not an option that appealed to him, but if he decided it was the best because it was the safest, he'd cross over to Canada and either remain there or fly out of there to a destination as yet undetermined. He had three excellent sets of forged papers, including a black American Express card that remained viable, which had been stored in his safe deposit box and which now resided in the side of a hollowed out tree thirty feet from where he stood. Each of them was more than adequate to get him safely in and out of Canada. I have an hour or two to decide, he thought to himself. Three hours at most. I must make my choice by no later than eight o'clock this evening.

In a related event, Sarah Ehrenson pulled her Mercedes SUV into the driveway of Cassandra Quick's niece's home just outside Ivanhoe, North Carolina, at exactly fifteen minutes after five o'clock on that very same evening. As she and her three passengers exited the car, they were now just over forty-five minutes away from where Eric Malanga was making his life-changing decision.

CHAPTER TWENTY FIVE

"I could really use a hot cup of coffee, black, if there is any," David Keating said to Beatrice Bush and Bart Clarkson.

"Bart, would you please call room service and tell them to put a rush on some fresh brewed coffee. Make sure it's one of their big pots. Have them send a plate of turnovers or doughnuts or brownies with it." Beatrice said.

"Perfect," Agent Keating said and slumped down gratefully on one of the big sofas in the oversized living room. "It's been a long day. I hit the road at four this morning. And I'm no spring chicken anymore." Beatrice Bush thought he looked about thirty five. But she said nothing while she gave him one of her best smiles.

"Let's wait for the coffee, shall we?" she said to the two of them. "That'll give Agent Keating a chance to relax and catch his breath. You were in Fayetteville?"

"I was," he said. "There was an incident at Fort Bragg where our assistance was requested."

"Oh?" Bart Clarkson said. "Are you often involved with military matters?"

"Not often," Keating said. "But if a civilian is involved, we tend to get a call."

The knock on the door broke into their conversation. Then a waiter wheeled a cart with a large coffer urn, a pitcher of milk, a bowl of sugar, cups and spoons and a plate of various pastries into the room. He left wheeling the cart with the remains of the earlier dinner.

David Keating poured himself a steaming cup of black coffee, took an apple pastry on a cocktail napkin and returned to the sofa where he placed his things on the coffee table in front of him. Neither Beatrice Bush nor Bart Clarkson joined him.

"So you're interested in Mickey Huntley," Keating said.

"We are indeed," Bea Bush replied.

"Is she involved with a case of yours," Keating asked.

"That's one of the things we're trying to determine,' she said.

"Uh huh," the FBI agent said. "Well, if she is be prepared to find yourselves, as I am very fond of saying to anyone who will listen, bamboozled; which is a jocular way of saying this woman is the smartest lawyer I know and she could stonewall Almighty God himself if she chose to."

"She is apparently involved with a woman named Sarah Ehrenson," Clarkson said.

"She sure is. They're lovers. And Ehrenson is frightening on the computer. She can find out anything about anybody. She's also thick as thieves with a pair of private investigators, Cash Delaney and Stella Conroy. So if your case dovetails with any of those names you have yourselves some serious challenges ahead." Keating took a big bite of the apple fritter and followed that with a good swig of coffee.

"What happened when you encountered them?" Bea Bush asked.

"For me, eventually, nothing. My case, and trust me when I tell you there was a case, died a very quiet death. For them, although I can't tell you the extent of their success, I know they accomplished whatever they set out to do and then they managed an extra bonus. We never found the man or woman responsible for two murders; nevertheless, I feel comfortable saying that I believe justice was somehow served. I simply have no idea how.

But I am still in the dark about just what their bonus was. Mickey Huntley was the front person for the entire caper and I never even got to first base with her. Did she break the law? I doubt it. Did she stand on the law and give me a dozen Bronx cheers along the way? Absolutely. But do I respect her. Yes. In fact, I respect all of them. And I still have no idea just what the ramifications were in the case I was given to investigate, because that case dovetailed in some way with whatever they were investigating. We called it closed simply because Mickey Huntley and team closed it when they closed their own."

"My god," Bea Bush said suddenly and glanced wide eyed at Bart Clarkson. "Where is Mickey Huntley's office located?"

"Oh, she's got a suite of offices on Front Street overlooking the river in Wilmington. Why?" It was David Keating who answered her.

"Who was surveilling the sister?" she asked Clarkson.

"Lenny," he said to her. "Why?"

Beatrice Bush didn't answer him. Instead she grabbed her cell phone, hit a button and when her call was answered, said "Lenny, you tailed Brooke Malanga for a day or two?"

"Yes," he said.

"Do I remember that you followed her to a building on Front Street in Wilmington?"

"That's right. A big office building. I figured she was visiting a client. Why?"

"Did you write down the building's address?"

"Sure. Give me a minute. I've got to look it up in my notebook. Here it is. 124 North Front Street. And boss, nobody's home at Conroy's house or that boat. I'm on my way to the husband's condo now."

"Phone when you finish," Beatrice Bush said; then she ended the call. "Bart, look up Mickey Huntley's address, please. There's a Wilmington City phone book in a drawer in my bedroom." But even as he went to do so, Bea Bush already thought she knew the answer.

"124 North Front Street," Clarkson hollered from the other room. Then he rejoined her and Agent Keating in the living room. The look on Beatrice Bush's face told him there was a story she was about to relate that he wouldn't want to listen to.

"The sister wasn't visiting a client, as we previously thought, when she went to that building on Front Street. She went to see Mickey Huntley. God damn it!" she said vehemently. "Brooke Malanga has engaged Mickey Huntley to search for her brother and the lawyer's been going about that business for several days now."

"Well, from that you can infer that Attorney Huntley undoubtedly enlisted the aid of her cohorts Delaney and Conroy. And they, in turn, included Ehrenson." David Keating said. "I'd advise you not to underestimate what Ehrenson has been able to find out about your own search at this point because it's undoubtedly more than you can tolerate."

Beatrice Bush was startled for a moment. "You know our business?" she said to him.

"I know the parameters," Keating said. "I know you're looking for someone you consider to be a rogue agent and I can guess that you think he has committed a crime."

"This is common knowledge?" Bart Clarkson asked him.

"You have visited a large number of local and county law enforcement agencies," Keating said. "Information like that finds it way around the legal community. But is it public knowledge? Absolutely not."

"This is a mess," Bea said, more to herself than to the men in the room. "These people have all disappeared; we have no idea where they've gone, but we have to assume they have learned of Malanga's whereabouts and are on their way to finding him."

"And there's one other thing you need to know that I have to admit makes no sense whatsoever," David Keating said to her. "My office routinely listens to and records an office landline phone in an antique business that is a front, albeit a profitable one, for a bigwig Wilmington drug lord. This man's name is Maurice Washington. His street name is Big Daddy. He was also some sort of a player in that case of mine that also involved Mickey Huntley and company. Both Delaney and Conroy visited him one afternoon and immediately following that visit the case very quickly ended. I couldn't even get an inkling of what, if any, part he played."

Bea Bush felt her head begin to spin. She knew she was on an information overload and she also knew she was experiencing a sudden drop in blood pressure. So she forced herself to get up out of the overstuffed armchair she was sitting in and walk slowly to the little bar to pour herself a glass of water. It seemed to disconcert Agent Keating. He just stopped talking.

"Please go on," she said as she poured a big glass of water for herself.

That seemed to bring Keating back to his senses. "Yes. Well, a few days ago I was manning that tapped line myself. A paid snitch of Washington's called him. Although the message was cryptic, the gist of it involved two sheriff's deputies shooting and killing an active duty marine they must have thought was this rogue agent y'all are looking for. And there's also been a total information blackout surrounding the incident. Washington then instructed the snitch to contact a friendly source from the New Hanover County Sheriff's Office. For some reason, Maurice Washington wanted his source to learn the name of your rogue agent. You should probably assume that by now he knows it."

If Beatrice Bush found this information startling in any way, she gave no indication of it. Instead, she let it simmer awhile in her brain while she drank the glass of water and walked back to the chair she'd previously been sitting in. Finally, she turned to Keating and said, "I don't think it means a thing to me or the agency; it might, however, mean something to you if you get close to an arrest of Mr. Washington."

Bart Clarkson couldn't help himself. He smiled sardonically and quietly muttered, "Leverage. It's golden as leverage. Jesus, Bea. This IS a fucking mess."

As the light dawned on David Keating and as the two CIA agents looked at each other, Beatrice Bush's cell phone rang again.

"Yes," she said.

"Lenny, boss. Nobody's home anyplace, anywhere, period. Instructions?"

"Drive to Topsail Beach," she said. "If the sister's home, arrest her. Call me when you arrive, whether she's there or not. I need to hear from you one way or another."

CHAPTER TWENTY SIX

Sheriff Billy Conroy was more agitated than Louise Dickson had ever seen him. There had been no one at Stella's house, and when Billy had let them in with his key, they'd found her cell phone on her small bedside table. It was turned off.

"This is unthinkable," Billy had muttered. "Stella never goes anywhere without she has her cell phone."

Louise hadn't been able to conjure anything to say that would mollify him, so she'd said nothing. When they'd pulled into the parking lot to access the Portofino, the sheriff looked crestfallen. "You sit tight. It won't take me a minute to see if he's on board," he said to her. Less than three minute later, he pulled out of the parking lot, saying only "Nope. It's uninhabited." When they got to Cooper Grey's condo, neither one of them said anything. What was there to say? Every one of the places they went to were empty. Everyone had simply disappeared.

It took Billy Conroy a mere twenty minutes to drive the usual half hour plus needed to get from Carolina Beach to Front Street in Wilmington because he activated his siren and cars scattered left and right to get out of his way. When he and Louise arrived at Mickey Huntley's office address there were no available parking spots. The sheriff double-parked his car, and he and Louise hurried into the still-occupied building. It was nearly six thirty when the two of them exited the elevator to the left of the lawyer's office suite. They could see light coming from inside the front room.

"Unless he leaves his lights on when he goes home, Darius is still inside," Louise said. "Or Mickey herself is." She sounded hopeful. They hurried to the door and when Billy opened it, for a moment they saw nothing but an empty room.

"Darius? Mickey?" Louise nearly shouted each name. Then they heard something fall and hit the floor and break apart. Then they saw a door open to reveal a small kitchen and then they each looked at Darius Millar. Sheriff Billy Conroy felt a sense of relief flood through his body as Mickey's young assistant said,

"That was a birthday gift to Mickey from Miss Sarah that is now lying in pieces all over the kitchenette floor. Boss'll have my hide for this. What in the world are you two doing here at this hour of the evening? Has somebody died?"

"We are looking for my daughter," Billy said.

"So y'all came here?"

"We're looking for Stella and Cash and Sarah and Cooper and Jefferson and your boss, Darius. They have all disappeared and trust me when I tell you that Billy is loaded with anxiety that could easily turn into a heart attack," Louise said to him. "Can you help us out? Do you know where they are?"

Darius Millar didn't answer her directly. Instead, he walked to his desk, picked up what looked like a tape recorder, fiddled with it for a minute and laid it back where it had previously been; then he said, "I'm going back to the kitchenette to clean up the mess I made. Won't take me more than a couple minutes. Y'all don't wanna be messing with anything while I'm gone. Have a seat." Then he winked at them and left the room.

Louise Dickson hustled over to face his desk and hit the play button on the tape recorder he'd activated. What she heard was a recording of Attorney Mickey Huntley's voice.

"We're in Ivanhoe, Darius. We have located Malanga and we'll be going to his location in an hour or so. Everybody's here. Nobody has a personal cell phone. Do not try to call any of us; it'll just go to voicemail and we don't want messages left. We will try to contact you on Skype as the hours pass to keep you updated on our progress, so carry your laptop with you at all times.

Brooke is going to join us shortly because I don't want the CIA to have access to her. Their interrogation techniques would break her. You, of course, know nothing except that I am arguing an amicus brief on a voting rights issue in Raleigh, and that is where I told you I would be. I did not tell you where because I do not wish to be disturbed. You know nothing about any of the others, none of whom you have seen in some time.

Additionally, I noticed last week that you have a lot of vacation time accrued. Now is the perfect moment for you to take a ten-day trip to wherever strikes your fancy. Be sure to send me a postcard. I'll see you when you get back."

When Darius walked back into his office, Billy and Louise were sitting in chairs fronting his desk. "I can't help you," Darius said politely. "I wish I could." The next moment, Billy and Louise watched him rewind and put the tape recorder in a briefcase that he always carried with him to and from the office.

"Understood," the Sheriff said. "I'm surprised you're even here at this hour."

"I'm just about to leave," he said, picking up the briefcase. "In fact, I'll walk out with you if you give me a minute. By the way, don't be surprised if I'm unavailable for a while. I'm taking a ten-day vacation." Darius Millar had a huge grin on his face when he uttered those words.

The three of them exited the building a few minutes later. They all shook hands. Darius turned to walk south on Front Street and Sheriff Billy Conroy and Louise Dickson returned to his cop car and drove out of Wilmington to return to Bolivia, passing Millar as they drove by. Billy had decided to become as unavailable to the CIA as everybody else was. He and Louise would each work from home until thing blew over, assuming it finally did.

As they entered Carolina Beach road heading out of Wilmington, and unbeknownst to them, an automobile driven by Bart Clarkson, with Beatrice Bush in the passenger's seat, turned south on Front Street and double-parked right where they had been in front of Mickey Huntley's office building.

––––––––––

Cassandra Quick and her cousin Cuddy took a little known alternate route to her niece's house in Ivanhoe and the two of them arrived ahead of the rest, even though they'd stopped at one of their favorite taverns for some fried catfish platters with coleslaw and double cooked fries and chilled sweet iced tea. When Cassandra pulled into her niece's long driveway it was a quarter to five.

"You decided when or if you're going to spill the beans about Sargasso to these people," Cuddy said to her.

"I have," she said to him. "But it can wait until we get Eric Malanga out of harm's way."

"Uh huh," Cuddy said. "Well, what with your nephew lyin' inside this house with a body so broken it will take a surgical miracle to even get him to the point where he can maybe sit up straight again, I hope the issue doesn't arise before you want it to."

"He's now in the locked wing that's attached to the six-car garage," she said. "None of the people who are joining us have any need to snoop in a house when their reason for being there is something not only pressing but entirely unrelated to that mission."

"And your niece knows to remain silent about it when she's around them?"

"She does indeed," Cassandra said. "But I don't want you thinking that I intend to simply confess my sins to these folks, Cuddy. I intend to enlist their help, up to and including that lawyer Mickey Huntley. I've got it in my mind she can get us the monetary and medical help that my nephew needs to begin a recovery. And do I believe she will give us that help? I most assuredly do. But first, we have to deal with Eric Malanga because he is actually at present in harm's way. Now let's go inside before my niece begins to wonder who the hell is sitting in her driveway, chatting."

Although he didn't admit it, Cudworth Sweat felt a sense of relief at Cassandra's last remarks. He'd had a worried mind that she might decide to just drop her efforts to ultimately force a showdown over the damage that had been done to their nephew once he'd ingested the drugs that had come from Sargasso Enterprises. The young man was just sixteen years old, and prior to his experiment with what they'd come to know as SOAR he'd been an outstanding member of his community: a good student, a fine athlete in both baseball and track, adept as a drummer and headed for a full scholarship at the University of North Carolina at Wilmington where he had been expected to major in criminal justice with an eye toward a law degree.

Everything had changed when the hallucinations the drug had caused in his brain led him to believe he could fly. And when he climbed a twenty-foot pine tree that stood on the far edge of his sister's backyard and jumped, the only thing that saved his life was a huge pile of lawn debris that had been raked the previous afternoon to be burned. He'd broken nearly every bone in his body and although the Lumbee tribe sent their best homeopathic healer who had tried to set the major breaks, as well as offer various spiritual healing ceremonies, nothing had healed correctly. Now he could not walk or even sit up. There would have to be countless conventional orthopedic surgeries performed on the teenager for him to begin any kind of meaningful rehabilitation.

But the family had no health insurance that would make such medical attention even partially possible. They made a bit too much money to be eligible for regular Medicaid, and because the controlling Republican legislature in North Carolina, along with the then Republican governor, had refused the federal Medicaid expansion to allow people to be able to afford to buy into what has become known as Obamacare, there was nothing to help them.

This was the situation that had driven Cassandra Quick and Cudworth Sweat to devise the plan to gaslight Paul Sargasso. They wanted to awaken and exacerbate his paranoia to the point where he would become susceptible to the idea that if he didn't help the broken young man, he would put himself at significant personal risk. In her heart, Cassandra had always believed it was a long shot. But she'd had to do something to right the wrong. Now, she saw another way. And she intended, when the time was right, to pursue it.

As they approached the sprawling house, Cassandra's niece opened the front door and ran to greet them. "I'm fixing rabbit stew," she said. "Petey asked for it. He looks better today, Cassandra."

"Good, good, good, Willow," Cassandra said to her niece whose given name was Frances. Everyone who knew her called her Willow. "Listen, I bring good news, as well. But first, you must prepare for visitors. We have a man's life we are obliged to save this evening."

"I got your message," Willow said. "Petey will remain unseen and unknown for now. But I am filled with hope for the first time in a long time."

"As you should be, niece," Cuddy said. "As you should be."

CHAPTER TWENTY SEVEN

The group decided to send Mickey Huntley and Brooke Malanga along with Cassandra Quick to rescue Eric Malanga from harm's way. So Coop and Jefferson quickly carried the eighteen-foot fishing skiff to the shore of the Black River, and a few minutes later the three women were motoring upstream to his nearly hidden campsite.

"Will he hear them coming," I said to Stella.

"Depends," she said. "Did Cassandra take a pair of oars with her, Coop?"

"A pair was attached and ready to go," he said.

"If she cuts the motor and uses the oars, then no, he won't hear them approach."

"That's exactly what she'll do," Cuddy said.

We were all sitting in overstuffed chairs or on couches in Willow Quick's living room. It was one of the largest living rooms I had ever seen. It must have been twenty-five feet wide and forty feet long, and the fireplace could have doubled as a parking lot for a couple of cars. The logs that were resting in it looked to be three deep and a good ten feet long.

"Who'd enjoy a cup of chamomile tea?" Willow asked. "I have a big pot steeping in the kitchen."

"My favorite tea," my partner said. "We'll all be grateful for a cup. Let me help you."

When Stella returned, she was carrying a tray with five mugs of tea and a large platter of what looked like oatmeal cookies. She was followed by Willow, who had her own mug and a dish of popcorn. I hadn't known I was hungry until I saw those cookies. But when I took a first bite of the raisin and walnut stuffed delight, I ate it so fast even Sarah noticed.

"Feel better?" she quipped and grinned at me.

"I guess I'm nervous," I said to her.

"I guess you're hungry," she answered.

Then we heard a phone ring and I realized we hadn't told either Coop or Jeff to turn their cell phones off. Cooper's cell was ringing.

"Don't answer that," Stella nearly yelled at him. "Just let it go to voicemail. Then turn it off. You, too, Jefferson. Turn yours off."

"It was your father," Cooper said to her. "You think he's the enemy?"

"I think his phone may be tapped or yours or Jeff's." she said. "He's probably tried to get in touch with me and can't because my phone is turned off and goes to voicemail. So he's worried. But he's going to have to be worried a tad longer. When the boat gets back, I'll have Sarah reach him; that's if his computer's on."

———————————————————————

"I'm going to dock the boat downstream from him and walk to his camp," Cassandra Quick said.

"Shouldn't I go with you?" Brooke Malanga said. "You might startle him into some sort of retaliation. I don't want you hurt."

175

"Your brother won't hurt me," she answered. "He's not violent. Here's a fine spot. We're probably a few hundred feet from his camp. I can smell the fire."

Although Mickey Huntley had her own reservations regarding what men who feel trapped will or won't do, she didn't interrupt Cassandra's plan except to say "You might let him know that his sister is a passenger in the skiff that brought you here."

Cassandra smiled at her. "I might," she said. When the skiff met the shore, she jumped out and quickly pulled it up far enough so that it held and then she tied it to a good-sized tree to secure it. Then she turned and headed for Eric Malanga's campsite. She was proceeding silently when she spotted him. He was drinking from a tin cup and the fire he'd started to cook his dinner was embers. He was in deep concentration when she said softly but clearly,

"Hello again, friend."

Eric Malanga was startled but simply turned his head to face the voice.

"You remember me?" Cassandra asked.

He looked at her until he finally said, "Were we on the river, fishing?"

"We were," she said. "Mind if I sit down? The fire, what's left of it, is welcoming."

"No," he said. "I don't mind. But if you're here to apprehend me, I'll have to warn you that I can't allow that to happen just yet. I won't hurt you but I will incapacitate you."

"I'm here to help you, Eric," Cassandra said. "Your sister and a top notch lawyer are waiting in the skiff I took to get here. And some crackerjack private investigators are also on board this train. We'll straighten this federal mess out. Shall we go?"

"My sister's here?" he said incredulously.

"She is," Cassandra said.

Eric Malanga stared at her. He was breathing through his mouth and his eyes were as big as saucers. "I don't believe you," is what he said.

"Why would I lie to you, Eric?" Cassandra asked. "How would I know you even have a sister?"

"People have been lying to me for years," he said bitterly.

"Yes, they probably have," she said. "But I'm not one of those people. Your sister is waiting for you in the rowboat I was fishing in when I first met you."

"Right now, I'm actually a little afraid of you," he said to her. "This is the exact way they'd trick me. Now it even makes a cold kind of sense: you work for them. They employ a fair number of stringers. So you put one and one together, got two, and now here you are. Our first meeting was anything but accidental. How long have they known how to trap me?" Eric Malanga stood up suddenly, kicked dirt over the embers of his fire to kill it, and began to walk away from Cassandra.

"Eric," a voice said, "Cassandra isn't your enemy. She's really your friend. And I'm your sister. Please don't leave. With the help of some very bright and fearless advocates, I finally remembered Ivanhoe and I've finally found you."

If there is such a thing as a peaceable heart, at that moment Eric Malanga finally trusted its embrace.

"I want an APB issued immediately on that Mercedes SUV that the Ehrenson woman drives. There can't be a lot of them in and around these parts. Notify every law enforcement agency in southeastern North Carolina," Beatrice Bush said to David Keating. She, along with Bart Clarkson, had returned to her suite at the Wilmington Hilton. "And please include the license plate number and a description of the passengers."

"Nothing at Mickey Huntley's office?" Keating asked. He was sitting in the FBI office in Wilmington, getting ready to go home.

"Correct," she said.

"I'll get on it," he said. "You want helicopters as well as police vehicles?"

"Not now. Order the helicopters at daybreak. For tonight, patrol cars will do."

"Any orders to attach?" Keating asked.

"Stop and detain for questioning by federal agencies," she said. "Remand to nearest law enforcement office and notify you at earliest convenience."

Keating was grateful for the inclusion. It didn't happen often enough, in his book. "Got it," he said.

"We'll be waiting to hear from you," Bea Bush said.

"Ten-four."

Billy Conroy could not sit still. He paced his house. He walked outside and paced his yard. A neighbor across the street who was pulling into his driveway saw him and felt a frisson of dread.

"Anything wrong, Billy?" the neighbor asked.

The sheriff looked at him. Then he realized the situation he was in. He was the law enforcement symbol of his community. He didn't have the same wide berth as his neighbors to express fear, a sense of alarm. He quickly gathered himself.

"Nothin' except a bit of nervousness about a date I am getting ready to go on, Denny. Y'all must remember what I'm frettin' about."

The tension left his neighbor. "You'll be fine, Billy," the man said. "You could charm a snake without a flute."

Billy Conroy smiled and saluted the neighbor. If only I could locate my daughter and her friends as easily as I fabricate I'd be copacetic, he thought to himself.

CHAPTER TWENTY EIGHT

"I'm a corporate lawyer," the man talking with Paul and Anthony Sargasso said; "I'm not prepared to advise you on criminal matters."

"No law's been broken," Anthony answered. The annoyance in his voice was obvious.

"Not yet," the lawyer said evenly. "But law enforcement's been attracted to your enterprise, and as a result you'll be under a microscope until you are either charged with something or you cease and desist."

"Surely you have a recommendation," Paul Sargasso said. He could feel tiny rivulets of sweat running down his rib cage. He glanced at his brother who looked to be completely devoid of tension of any kind.

"Let me put it this way," the man answered. "If I'd been warned by a North Carolina sheriff, personally, that the DEA had been notified of one of my businesses and would be taking an up-close and personal look at that business, I would cease and desist five minutes after that sheriff left my property. And in your case, because it's Billy Conroy, I might have thrown in the towel the second he was gone. While it's true that this state has its share of ersatz sheriffs,

Conroy isn't one of them. He's the real deal. In my opinion, he actually did you a favor by notifying you at all."

Paul Sargasso looked from the lawyer to his brother. Finally, he said, "You heard the man, Anthony. Cease and desist. As of this very moment your venture has ended. At least it has as far as this property is concerned."

Eric Malanga was overwhelmed by the sudden upheaval of his circumstances as well as by the number of people gathered in Willow Quick's home who were acting on his behalf. Who could blame him? He had been living in his own solitary confinement for a very long time. But we were still operating under a clock, and decisions had to be made. I pulled Mickey Huntley aside and said quietly, "We need to know if he killed Woodrow Keats; and if he did what the circumstances were. I'm disinclined to ask him this in a crowded living room. But until we know the answer we really can't proceed. And of course there's still good reason to believe that time is of the essence, whether he did it or not."

"I don't necessarily want to be involved in that conversation," Mickey said to me. "Eric may well need a lawyer at some future date and, in case that turns out to be me, the less I know about possible criminal liability the better."

"Okay," I said. Stella had noticed the two of us talking and sauntered over to join us.

"What's goin' on?"

"You and I are about to find out if Eric had a hand in Keats death," I said to her.

"Is that a euphemistic way of sayin' we need to know if he murdered him?" she asked. "Because it's more or less a given that he played some part in that unfortunate demise just by showing up back here when the CIA had written him off as a mere piece of missing or dead collateral."

I laughed out loud. "Yes," is what I said to her.

Eric Malanga was sitting on one of the sofas in the living room and talking with his sister. He was also eating one of those raisin and nut stuffed oatmeal cookies with the same rapidity I had earlier exhibited. A pitcher of milk and a half-full glass rested on the coffee table in front of him. Stella and I approached the two of them.

"We've got a couple of questions, Eric. Can you give us a minute?" I asked.

He looked at me. Then he looked at Stella. Then he smiled. "You bet I can," he said. At that exact moment I wanted to believe Cassandra Quick's assessment: Eric Malanga had not murdered Woodrow Keats. The softness and the sadness in the man's eyes had me wanting to agree with her: he wasn't violent.

"Let's walk outside for a bit, Eric," my partner said.

The man seemed to think about that request for a second or two. But then he stood up, handed what was left of his cookie to his sister and nodded his head. Brooke was looking beseechingly at me so I gave her a not-to-worry look. When the three of us reached the front porch and were all leaning on various parts of the side rails, I said, "Woodrow Keats is dead, Eric. Do you know anything about that?"

The news seemed to shock him and his immediate response was simply silence. When he did respond, all he said was, "Woody's dead? When? How?"

"That's the sixty-four-thousand-dollar question," Stella said to him. "Y'all remember when you saw him last? That's if you saw him at all."

"Oh, I saw him," Eric Malanga said. "Maybe ten or twelve days ago. Thereabouts anyway. I tracked him to Lejuene. It's his favorite recruitment site. It's where he first recruited me. But I also knew he would never stay overnight on base. He's got a place in Kure Beach where he summers. It's a fairly easy power walk from Ivanhoe to Kure. It took me a little less than eight hours."

"You went to his home?" I asked skeptically.

"No. I knew enough about Woody to be able to guess where he'd go for dinner," Eric said. "He's divorced, he lives alone, and he's a big fan of the double pork chops at Freddie's. So I sat on one of the benches that the town provides on the narrow median strip facing the place. He walked out around 9 p.m. There was only about fifteen feet between us. So I called out to him and asked him how he'd been.

I guess you'd be inclined to say I startled the man. For a minute or two I don't think he even recognized me. Then, his face actually drained of color and I watched him gauge his chances of avoiding me completely, one way or another. I knew he was probably armed. Unless he was in bed asleep he almost always was. But the little streets were busy and all of the shops were still open and bright. So he finally decided to cross the street and talk to me."

"Well, Keats hadn't been in the ocean all that long then when he paid us a visit," Stella said to me. I nodded.

"Then what happened?" I asked Eric Malanga.

"It wasn't a pleasant conversation," he said to me. "I was asking him real questions and he was reciting Agency protocols back to me. After a while, I realized this was all he was ever going to say: boiler plate rhetoric in the face of an actual human disaster. So my questioning stopped and all I said was that I intended to tell my story to someone influential who would listen, regardless of the effect it might have on me or the CIA. I owed Anjay at least that much.

I knew the risk I was taking to say that to him, but I honestly didn't care. He easily could have arrested me; for that matter, if he was armed, he could have shot me. I was, after all, threatening one of our national security agencies. But he did nothing except look at me with two tired eyes. Finally, when the silence became unbearable to me, I got up and walked away. And Woody let me. In retrospect, that choice probably cost him. But that was what he did. I never saw him again."

"So you didn't kill Keats," I said, more to myself than to anybody.

"No ma'am," he said to me. "And on my walk back to Ivanhoe, I stopped at two or three places to pick up some apples, to use the restroom, and at one place I bought a sweatshirt because the wind had picked up and I was cold. But if the CIA thinks I did it really won't matter. Besides, I'm a liability to them one way or another. They can probably make a case for me being the proximate cause of Woody's death. I'm not the first agent they've identified as rogue and retired quietly."

I looked at Eric Malanga and wondered what choices he would make at this point in his journey for justice. There was a part of me that didn't really want to know. Another part, however, needed answers. As I was resolving my dilemma, Stella Conroy said,

"So are y'all still hell bent on broadcasting your story?"

The bluntness of her question caught him off guard. Finally, he said heatedly, "Broadcasting my story? Is that what you think I'm doing?"

"My partner is just trying to gauge the parameters of your intent," I said hurriedly. "Are you thinking about telling your story to a congressional committee, to the Washington Post, or to some other, perhaps less reputable news organization?"

"This isn't about me," Eric Malanga said to me. "This is about my fiancé Anjay. Do you have any idea what they did to her because they believed she was working with me?"

"No," I said. "I don't. But you can believe me when I tell you that I've seen things that will haunt my dreams forever."

Eric didn't even register my response. By now, his eyes were brimming with tears and his voice was thick with grief. "They tortured her for two weeks before they finally killed her. And how did they finally kill her? They burned her alive. These people are immune to mercy." His sobs by now were racking his body and he was doubled over, hugging himself, trying to get back under control. He had finally given in to the grief that drove him. I moved to him and slowly rubbed his back and his arms while he gulped for air.

"Sit down for a minute," I said quietly to him, "and hug your knees. You'll feel a little better." Stella had moved a porch chair behind him and I eased him into it.

The door we had taken to get to the back porch opened and Sarah Ehrenson looked first at me then at Stella and finally rested on Eric. "I'm sorry to interrupt," she said, "but I just intercepted an FBI alert. A BOLO is in effect for my vehicle along with an order to detain and transport passengers to the nearest local law enforcement agency pending interrogation by a federal law enforcement agency."

I looked at Stella. She was lighting a cigarette and she might have been getting ready to order takeout from a restaurant, as far as her facial expression was concerned. When she'd taken a first deep drag on the cigarette, she looked at me and smiled.

"If ever we needed a blue moon, my friend, I'd say we could not have picked a choicer moment," she said. "Bein' hunted by both the FBI and the CIA makes me seriously consider my sanity."

Eric Malanga sat up straight and wiped his eyes, took out a cloth from one of his pockets and blew his nose. Then he stood up and walked back towards the living room. "I'm the cause of all of this," he said to the three of us. "This is my fight; no one else should be put at risk on my behalf. I appreciate all that you've done but I'm putting an end to this. Just give me a few minutes to speak with my sister and I'll be out of your lives forever."

He was met at the living room door by Mickey Huntley. "There is a way out if this unfortunate situation that will ultimately benefit everyone including you and your sister, Eric." the lawyer said. "And the best part of that is there's nothing really illegal about it. It will take a while to explain, and right now we need to pack up and leave Ivanhoe.

We'll be going to Cassandra Quick's home in Elrod. That's about an hour's drive and we'll be on a lot of unlit back country roads. Willow has agreed to let us leave the Mercedes in one of her garage spaces, which gets it out of sight and which she'll lock. We all can fit in Cooper's and Cassandra's cars. So let's get moving."

"Sure as hell feels like that once in a blue moon moment just showed up," Stella said quietly to me. Who knows? Maybe all the good guys'll finish first for a change."

"I'd put the odds of that materializing at fifty-fifty," I said to her.

"Better than zero," she said.

Who could argue with that?

CHAPTER TWENTY NINE

"Boss," Moses said to Maurice Washington, "FBI's got a car outside. Whaddya want I should do. Anything?"

Big Daddy, who had been doing the books on his various street activities, looked up at his nephew. "How many are there?" he asked. He was already sorting possibilities and consequences.

"Two. I saw them drive up and park maybe fifteen minutes ago. One's got a camera. No chatter on the street; it's a real quiet day. If somethin' big was about to hit my phone be lit up."

"When was the last time they pulled this stunt?" Big Daddy asked. By now, he was up out of his chair and filing the paper work he'd been doing. It was filed under "mergers and acquisitions," a choice that always amused him.

"Any serious surveillance? They went a month after that time Alvie was here with those two broads." His nephew said. "That Keating nearly drove me nuts. He's the big cheese over at the local FBI. But it ain't him this time. It's two suits I don't recognize. We in real trouble this time, boss?"

Maurice Washington weighed his options. On the one hand, if the federal authorities had caught up with him on some charge or other, his recent leverage might be very useful. On the other, if all this was merely a fishing expedition, they were nothing for him to worry about. He placed his bet on the second option.

"Let's give them a tour of some of our property acquisitions on the south side of town," he said to Moses. "Go get the car and take your cousin with you. Pick me up in five minutes at the back door. Then drive around the block and go right past them, see if they follow. If they do, we'll have a little fun."

Anthony Sargasso was also weighing possibilities and consequences. If he was being honest with himself, and he almost always was, he'd admit that he was as interested in the chemistry of his business as he was in the profitability. But he was also beginning to appreciate the power of money. And then there was a need to consider the wishes of his older brother. He had known for a while now that Paul's tolerance for risk was a good deal lower than his. He himself enjoyed the risk, and he appreciated the game of what amounted to little more than cat and mouse: whenever the law began to close the gap between safe and unsafe, he'd tweak a chemical formula to keep his enterprise legal. He was confident in his ability to win. But Paul didn't share his confidence. So he'd have to move his lab to neutral quarters and sooner rather than later.

Anthony was packing up his lab as he thought about his situation. It was a chore and a half to move his headquarters, and he'd miss a deadline for his customers unless he could accomplish it in a day or two. Then he remembered a name that a buyer of his from Wilmington had given him: Maurice Washington. He'd saved it in his Rolodex. The kid had told him if he ever wanted to set up a satellite lab to give this guy a call. Anthony seemed to recall the kid had also hinted that Washington himself was a drug dealer of some sort. But that didn't worry Anthony. He didn't compete with actual dealers. His wasn't an illegal shop—at least until if and when it was.

He reached for his Rolodex to find the number for Maurice Washington. A 910 area code. He thought that would be Wilmington. Then Anthony reached for his cell phone and dialed.

"Talk to me," said a rather deep cultured voice.

"My name is Anthony Sargasso," he said.

"And how may I help you," the voice asked pleasantly.

"I understand you have a certain number of commercially zoned properties for rent," Anthony said.

"I do indeed. Are you in the market for one?"

"Yes."

"Please outline your needs," the voice said.

"I'm a chemist so I need laboratory space, a finite heat source, a finite fire source and a reception area quite separate from the laboratory. I also require two work stations in the lab. One for myself and one for my assistant. I have no need for street visibility. I'm not in sales."

Big Daddy Washington smiled to himself and looked around at the small commercial building he was standing in. He figured it would be perfect for this man's needs. And at $5000.00 a month rent plus, he'd clear $60,000 a year for a building he'd purchased from Wells Fargo on the cheap because of a bad neighborhood and a foreclosure with no minimum at which he was the only bidder.

"I'm standing in a building that may be perfect for your work," he said. "It's rather small, two thousand square feet with a small office area of four or five hundred square feet attached. Where are you at the moment?"

"In Brunswick County," Anthony Sargasso said. "Where are you?"

"Just south of Eighth Street in Wilmington. 12 Wilson's Alley to be exact."

"Might you be there in an hour or so?"

"That can be arranged. By the way, what is your name again?"

"I'm Anthony Sargasso. And are you Maurice Washington?"

"I am."

"I look forward to meeting you, Mr. Washington."

"As do I you, Mr. Sargasso."

Tallahassee Bodine was picking grapes and watching Anthony Sargasso as he walked from his laboratory in the big barn to his car. The kid was carrying his briefcase and what looked like some sort of small tool box. So Tally called Junior Fisk. It was 4 o'clock in the afternoon.

"What?" Junior said irritably.

"Come down with a migraine now. Then pick me up. The chemist's on the move."

"Moody'll know y'all are gone too."

"You're my ride. I ain't got a choice."

"Be ready."

Five minutes later, Junior stopped and picked up his friend. "He's got a head start," he said.

"He also got a GPS tracker underneath his rear end," Tally said. "He ain't out of our sight." He flipped a switch on a tracking device Cooper Grey had given him and the moving blip showed Anthony Sargasso heading for Shallotte. "Let's hit it, make up some time on him. He ain't but a few minutes ahead of us."

Forty minutes later, as they were crossing the Cape Fear Memorial Bridge into Wilmington, Tally said, "Don't follow him too close on some of these city side streets, Junior. Be way too easy to pick us up as a tail if y'all do."

"Where the hell's he goin'," Junior said.

"He headin' right into the South side of the city," Tally said. "Look out. He's turnin' in a little alleyway offa Eighth Street. Drive right by and park. We can circle back on foot."

A few minutes later, the two of them watched as Anthony Sargasso pulled his sports car into a parking slot in front of a commercial building that was undergoing a renovation. The sign in front of the site was billboard size. It read as follows: "Another project brought to you by Maurice Washington Associates. We work to restore the south side of Wilmington to its former thriving status. Reach us at 1-800-555-9892."

"Holy shit," Junior Fiske exclaimed. "The kid's on his way to see Big Daddy."

"Yes indeedy do," Tally said as he snapped several photos of the two men shaking hands before they turned and disappeared from view. When he'd finished, he sent the iPhone photos to Cooper Grey with this text message: "The kid just met Big Daddy outside a shop looks to be for rent offa Eighth Street in Wilmington. What now, Coop?"

I was actually exhausted, and it was the last way I should have been feeling. We were somewhere in a North Carolina county called Robeson that I had never heard of, let alone visited. It was a little before ten o'clock on a moonlit night and all I wanted to do was take a shower and sleep. Instead, we were all rail sitting on a porch where two rocking chairs held no promise whatsoever for the size of the crowd that had gathered there.

Stella and I had sent Coop and Jefferson on their way, and they'd decided to stop off and inspect their oyster beds before returning home to Carolina Beach. I had urged Cooper to remain available should we need him, and he had agreed. So here we were. The front door of the small house opened and Sarah emerged carrying a huge tray of plastic cups, a sugar bowl, a quart of milk and a pot of coffee. When everybody had poured a cup, she said to Stella and me, "I need to see you for a minute inside."

So we three walked into the living room. I noticed her computer was set up on the coffee table. "I just saw this email from Coop," is what she said to the two of us. "He sent it a while ago. Take a look." The message that each of us read was this: "Tally and Junior tailed the brother to this location off 8th Street in Wilmington. I'm stumped. Please advise." The three photos followed.

Stella looked at the pictures and then looked at me. "What the fuck?" she said.

"I have no idea," I said.

"That makes two of us," she said.

"He's asking for instructions," Sarah said. "You'll have to think of something."

"Hard to instruct when you've got no idea what's going on," Stella said.

"Say this," I said to Sarah. "Coop: have Tally and Junior continue to monitor the brother and his new situation for the next day or so. Their jobs at the vineyard are no longer important. The kid is. And we will probably need you to pick us up tomorrow morning, pending unforeseen developments. I'll call you before 7 tomorrow morning."

"Do you want both of the boys to come to get us?" Sarah asked.

"No. Coop is fine by himself." I said.

At that moment, Cassandra Quick, her cousin Cuddy, and Mickey Huntley walked into the room to join us. "Something else has come up," our lawyer said. "We need to talk about it and decide how to proceed."

"Jesus Christ, what now?" Sarah said under her breath.

We were about to discover those aforementioned unforeseen developments.

CHAPTER THIRTY

"We have a situation," Mickey Huntley said to the three of us. "I'd call it dicey but containable."

"If you call it dicey," Sarah said, "I suspect the three of us might well call it dangerous." Cassandra Quick's face suddenly blushed bright red. I couldn't help but notice.

"Something on your mind, Cassandra?" I asked.

"Yes," she said.

"Let's hear it," said Stella.

"It's complicated," Cuddy said imploringly.

I sighed deeply. "My middle name is complicated," I said. Mickey Huntley smiled.

"Cassandra and her cousin are the persons responsible for the damage to Paul Sargasso's vineyards." the lawyer said. "There are extenuating circumstances."

"There always are," Stella muttered. Again, Mickey smiled.

"So we're dealing with a quid pro quo?" asked Sarah, looking directly at Mickey.

"Obliquely," Mickey said.

"No," Cassandra said emphatically. "If you're suggesting I helped y'all in exchange for your aid with my situation you're dead wrong. I would have helped you regardless. But I am obliged to share with you my responsibility for the damage to Sargasso's vineyards. I come from a long line of honorable people. We've been defeated in battle but we've never been ethically compromised."

"Cassandra's 16-year-old nephew is effectively a paraplegic," Mickey said. "That's the result of a friend sharing with him some of the legal concoction that Anthony Sargasso is peddling. The boy thought he could fly from the top of a tree beside his home—the home we just left to come here--and decided to prove it. The result, of course, was catastrophic.

The family has a woeful lack of medical insurance, insufficient to cover the multiple surgeries his condition requires. This prompted the vandalism to the vineyards. If this strikes anyone as fruitless, consider the value of induced paranoia. But I digress. This situation, after all, will not include a discussion of psychology. There's a wrong to be righted and I intend to pursue it."

"There's more than one wrong to be righted here, Mickey. Stella and I are deputized members of North Carolina law enforcement, specifically for this particular case," I said. "That isn't something either one of us can simply dismiss. Billy will have to be informed."

"And I intend to inform him," Mickey said. "Will you two weigh in at all?"

"Of course we will," I said.

"Y'all know perfectly well that daddy's always has a soft spot for the suffering of children," my partner said.

I looked at Stella. "Might be a good idea to give your father a call." I said to her.

"Right now?" She asked.

"Do you have a landline," I said to Cassandra Quick.

"Yes."

"Okay then. Yes, right now," I said to Stella.

"That Mercedes must have been swallowed up by a sinkhole," David Keating said to Beatrice Bush. They were talking over what Keating had assured her was a secure line. "It's disappeared off the face of the earth."

"More likely that the Ehrenson woman intercepts our communications somehow and so they all remain a few steps ahead of us," Beatrice answered. "No doubt she's parked it where it can't be seen. Does Conroy have a garage at her house?"

"Yes, but we checked it. It's full of furniture and stuff," said Keating.

"Check all the local storage units," she said.

"One of our agents is calling them now."

Bart Clarkson walked into the living room of the Hilton suite and ran his finger across his throat. "Hang on a minute, David," Beatrice said. "Is there news?" She said to Clarkson.

"Lenny called. Grey and Davis are back in Carolina Beach. He's waiting on instructions."

"Don't those two always wind up on that massive boat that Davis owns?"

"That's been the pattern we've observed,' he said. Beatrice Bush said into her cell phone, "Let me call you back in a little bit, David. We may have a line on something important."

When she'd ended the call, she turned back to Clarkson and said, "I bet they're all going to be landing back on that boat. And Malanga may well be with them. Access to water might be the safest way to get him away from us. I'll alert the Coast Guard. Have Lenny stay there and continue to monitor Davis. I'll send another agent to join him and they can divide the monitoring duty between Davis and Grey. And for god's sake have him keep us informed."

When Sheriff Billy Conroy walked into the Brunswick County Sheriff's Office a little after eleven o'clock, Louise Dickson was already there. She was sitting at her desk drinking a cup of coffee and reading a bunch of police reports. She looked up when she heard the front door opening.

"What's the emergency, Billy, that couldn't wait until morning?" she asked.

"I could well be indicted by tomorrow morning for what I'm about to do," he said. "You may not want to be involved. And Louise, I will completely understand if that's what y'all decide is best for you."

Louise said nothing. She had known Billy Conroy for what seemed like forever and she knew he had a weakness for what can only be called the dramatic. And although she knew he occasionally welcomed what he called the accidental omission of evidence, at this moment she couldn't recall him ever suggesting he was about to knowingly break the law. Finally, she managed, "Well, okay. Let's hear it."

"Stella and Cash are on their way here as we speak. I expect them any minute now. They're bringin' some other folks along includin' Mickey and Sarah and the two people responsible for the damage to those damned vineyards in Little Prong."

"So far all you've told me is that we've solved a case," Louise said.

"Uh huh. There's a tad more. They're also bringin' that Malanga fella the Feds are chasin' that we all suspect they'll kill, they find him. His sister isn't with him. She's layin' low in a house the Feds don't know about in Ivanhoe."

"Oh my," she said.

"I've agreed to hide him in one of our empty cells for a few days on a charge of vagrancy so Mickey can work her magic, likely save his life."

"I see" she said and paused. "Well, that does present multiple chances of being charged with various felonies. I think there's a new bottle of Jim Beam in your office, Billy, and I am going to need something a bit stronger than coffee right now. Do you mind?"

"Mind? Hell, I insist."

"Then I'll stay," she said. "Y'all know I'm an in for a penny in for a pound kind of girl. Seems silly to change my way of thinking now."

Sheriff Billy Conroy hoped Louise Dickson didn't notice the huge wave of relief that swept over him when those were the words she chose to utter.

Tallahassee Bodine was certain that the raucous snoring that was emanating from Junior Fisk could be heard by anyone who was still awake within a five-mile radius from where they were parked and waiting upon developments from Anthony Sargasso. When they'd pulled off the road a half mile below the barn laboratory at nine o'clock that night, there'd been only one small outside light on. Now there were multiple lights on inside as well. He looked at his watch. Eleven o'clock. Junior'd been sleeping for the past hour and showed no signs of stopping. And neither did his snoring. But it was still 75 degrees outside and Tally couldn't bring himself to close the cars windows. They'd sweat to death.

He opened the car door to get out and stretch his legs just as a U-Haul truck passed them heading towards the barn. When it reached that structure, the truck pulled in and disappeared behind it. Tally eased back into the car and shook Junior's shoulder.

Junior snorted, opened his eyes and said loudly "Say what?!?"

"They loadin' a U-Haul at the lab. Might could be about to head on back to that warehouse Big Daddy got in Wilmington."

"I was sleepin'," Junior said dyspeptically.

"No kiddin'," Tally said. "Couple corpses rose up outta that graveyard across the road."

"Y'all accusing me of snorin'?"

"I wounded a warthog, he be more quiet than you Junior. Here comes the truck. Duck down."

"You take that back, Tally," Junior said. His head was underneath the steering wheel. His rump was aimed directly at Tally.

"Start the car, Junior. U-Haul's passed us."

"Take it back. I ain't no warthog. I lost another three pounds this week," he said stubbornly.

Tallahassee Bodine sighed. "Okay, okay. I take it back," he said. His hands were out of sight. On both of them his fingers were crossed.

CHAPTER THIRTY ONE

"Lenny called," Bart Clarkson said through a crack in the bathroom door. Beatrice Bush was up to her chin in a bubble bath that permeated the entire room with the smell of roses. She was also listening to a beautiful Mozart sonata she hadn't heard for a while, and the tea she was drinking was her absolute favorite: lemon hibiscus. Although she had told Clarkson to keep her updated, she realized she deeply resented this intrusion on her meditation of bliss. But duty was duty. She turned down the volume until the strains of the Sonata were barely audible.

"And?" she said.

"We missed Grey. By the time our agent reached his condo, he was gone. Must have left shortly after we last talked with Lenny."

"Did he leave without Davis?" she asked.

"Yes. Mr. Davis is still aboard his yacht."

After a rather pregnant pause, Bea Bush said, "Take whatever pantsuit is clean and pressed out of my closet, along with a black cotton turtleneck in the top drawer of the dresser, and lay it all out for me on my bed. Then go gas up the car and drive it around front. I'll meet you in fifteen minutes. We need to see what Davis has to say about this whole damned shebang. And we need to do it before he disappears as well."

Forty five minutes later, they pulled into the parking lot closest to the town marina where Jefferson Davis moored The Portofino. As they approached the boat, they could clearly see a man sitting in a lounge chair with his back to them. He was on the aft deck.

"Hello the boat," Bart Clarkson said rather loudly. The man in the deck chair turned to peer at them.

"Are y'all addressin' me?" he asked.

"We are if you're Jeff Davis," Beatrice Bush said.

"That's me," Jefferson said, realizing he had seen one of these two people before and also realizing it was in conjunction with the search for Eric Malanga. He knew he needed to be at his best when he talked with them.

"Permission to come aboard," Clarkson said.

"It's eleven o'clock at night," Jeff said amiably. "I'm about to retire."

"Mr. Davis," Beatrice Bush said, "I'm Special Agent Beatrice Bush from the CIA. I suspect you already know Agent Clarkson from an earlier interview. Either you cooperate with me now or I will impound your vessel in the name of national security."

Jeff Davis was inwardly smiling. But to Beatrice Bush he offered a look of alarm. "Why?" is what he said.

"You have no need to know," she said.

"It's my home you're threatening to impound," he said. "And I have no need to know why?"

"Correct," she said.

"I guess I'll need to call my lawyer," Jeff said. "If y'all will excuse me a moment." He turned away from them and reached for his cell phone. Then he walked out of their hearing range on the far side of the aft deck and dialed a number.

"Brunswick County Sheriff's Office," Louise Dickson said.

"I have got Beatrice Bush and one of her agents saying they'll impound my boat if I refuse to talk with them," Jeff said. "Guidance would be most welcome."

"I see. Hold please."

Thirty seconds later, Mickey Huntley said, "Let them impound it. You know nothing regarding whatever it is they want to talk with you about and have been advised to remain silent on the advice of counsel. You also cannot be compelled to identify your counsel. Neither can they board the boat without your permission or a warrant, which I suspect they don't have at the moment and won't be able to get until tomorrow morning. And Jeff, when you end this call, stumble a bit and toss your phone overboard, as far away from the boat as you can manage. Otherwise, they'll be able to trace who you called. I'll be in touch no later than seven o'clock tomorrow morning. Can you do that?"

"Of course," he said. "They'll probably be sending somebody to Coop's house if they haven't already done it. Might be good to get him out of town." In a somewhat louder voice he said, "Thanks." Then, as he turned, he tripped over a foot stool and landed with his stomach against the guardrail. His phone went flying across the roiling water. "God damn it," he said heatedly. After kicking the foot stool halfway across the aft deck of the boat, he gathered himself and returned to talk with his visitors.

"Please do not board my boat but feel free to impound it," is what he said. "I am tired, it's late, and I'm goin' to bed. So if y'all will excuse me, I'll say goodnight."

Stella and I were in Louise Dickson's car just inside the Kure Beach town line. A few minutes later, we slid the car into one of the parking spaces in front of Freddie's, the restaurant where Woodrow Keats had dinner the night he spoke with Eric Malanga. It was twelve thirty in the morning but when we walked into Freddie's the little place was still jumping.

We finally scored two barstools closest to the door to the kitchen. When the bartender idled over to take our order, I said, "You mind if I ask you a question?"

"Shoot," he said.

"Do you know Woodrow Keats?"

"Woody? Everybody around here knows him. Why?"

"You remember when y'all saw him last," Stella said.

The young man looked up at the ceiling. He was tapping his fingers rapidly on the bar. One of the waiters walked up and slapped the wooden ledge to get his attention. "I need two gin martinis three olives each and a vodka tonic double lime, Matt."

The bartender's head snapped back and he began building the drinks. "When was Woody Keats in here last," he said to the waiter.

"'Bout two weeks ago," the waiter said. "He ate dinner and left but then he came back, which is why I remember. He got so drunk we had to help him out. We basically carried him and sat him down on the park bench across the street and called a cab to come pick him up. Why?"

"Two friends of his are looking for him," bartender Matt said.

"If he's not around here he's most likely at Lejeune," the waiter said. He placed the three drinks on his tray and walked away.

"Do you happen to recall what Cab Company you called?"

"Art's," Matt said immediately. He's in Carolina Beach and he's reliable. You want his number?"

"Yes please," I said.

"And we'll have a couple muddled bourbon old-fashioneds and a couple shrimp cocktails while we're here," Stella said to him.

"Yes ma'am," he said to her, and grinned while he handed me a business card that read "Pleasure Island Shutter-Cab" and a phone number. I dialed the number on the phone Mickey had purchased at Best Buy.

"Art's," said a pleasant male voice.

"I'm trying to locate a friend of mine," I said. "I'm in Freddie's Restaurant in Kure Beach and the bartender told me he called you to pick up a man named Woody Keats a couple of weeks ago. I wonder if you could tell me where you dropped him off."

"I could if I'd actually dropped him off someplace," the man said.

"He didn't get in your cab?" I said.

"He wasn't anywhere around when I got there. I drove around that block twice looking for him cause Matt told me he was shi..., excuse me, blotto. I've picked Woody up several times this year and I was surprised I couldn't find him. I've really never known him to be a big drinker. But we do get our fair share of inebriated people most nights in the summertime. And that night, he was a no show. I figured he must have staggered home."

"I see," I said. "Well, thank you, sir."

"Name's Art," he said cheerfully. "You ever need a ride, call me." And he ended the conversation.

I took a good sip of the ice cold old fashioned in front of me, and picked up one of the jumbo shrimp to dip into the cocktail sauce. I chewed it slowly to savor the freshness of the seafood. "Well," I said to Stella, "we've got two choices. First is a suicide. Keats was overwhelmed by guilt and flung himself into the Atlantic and drowned. Second is an accident. Keats decided to walk home, was incredibly impaired, stumbled down the street instead of up and fell off the end of the pier and drowned. Take your pick."

"Incredibly impaired," Stella said softly. "That appeals to me. I choose trap door number two, Monty."

"He retired." I said.

"So did Woodrow Keats," my partner said.

CHAPTER THIRTY TWO

"Y'all are tellin' me two sheriff's deputies from Pender County shot and killed an active duty marine with a wife and four children 'cause they thought he was this guy here?" Billy Conroy said to Mickey Huntley while pointing at Eric Malanga.

"Yes," the lawyer said.

"It ain't hit any airwaves I'm familiar with," the sheriff said skeptically, "and murders tend to do that."

"The CIA has it on blackout," Sarah said. "The story given to Lejeune and everybody else is that this marine died in a shootout with fugitive Eric. So now, the CIA has chosen an actual murder to pin on him. The marine was given a hero's funeral and his family will be taken care of by the government. The widow has expressed an interest in remaining at Lejeune, where other family members and many friends also reside."

"Haskell Shorter must be tearin' his hair out," Billy said. "Those yahoos from the Feds have been all over these parts for a few days now tellin' us to be on the lookout for you," he said, staring directly at Eric. "But they also told us specifically not to do anything but follow and notify them. They wanted the arrest, which was fine with me."

"Apparently, Sheriff Shorter didn't get the memo."

"Ignored it, more likely," Louise said. "Lejeune's in his county. He's very protective."

Billy's landline phone rang. Louise reached for it. "Brunswick…" she managed.

"It's me, Louise," Stella Conroy said. "Might as well put it on speaker, save unnecessary repetition."

"Done," said Louise.

"Well, I reckon we've got ourselves an accident to contend with when it comes to the death of Woodrow Keats," Stella said laconically.

"Where are you?" Mickey asked.

"We're each enjoyin' a shrimp cocktail and a bourbon old fashioned at Freddie's," Stella said.

"I am in no mood for frivolity," the sheriff said to his daughter.

"Woody Keats did have dinner at Freddie's two weeks ago," Cash Delaney said. "He did leave that restaurant, did see and speak with Eric Malanga that evening, did watch Eric walk away, and then rather than go home himself, he went back into Freddie's and drank himself silly, and at closing time was carried back to the bench he had earlier shared with Eric to wait for a cab the staff of Freddie's had called for him; but he wasn't there when the cab arrived. So he was either a suicide jumper off the Kure Beach Town Pier or an accidental drowning due to disorientation from excessive alcohol consumption. We chose the latter. Your choice is up to you."

"Poor Woody," Eric Malanga said quietly. "It's true I wanted him to feel the real cost of collateral damage. But I didn't want him to actually define it by dying."

"Thank you for waiting to speak with Sheriff Conroy," Louise Dickson said to Cassandra Quick and Cudworth Sweat. "Would either of you like a coffee?"

"We're both okay," Cuddy said.

"Then if you'll just follow me," Louise said and headed back into Billy's office.

When the three of them had all taken seats around the small conference table in front of the picture window, Billy Conroy smiled at each of them and said, "So, Attorney Huntley tells me she's representin' y'all and you'd like to turn yourselves in on three counts of misdemeanor vandalism, specifically relating to the loss of property at Paul Sargasso's vineyard."

"Correct," Cassandra Quick said. "Did our attorney include our truly heartfelt explanation for breakin' the law?"

"She did. And I am sympathetic. But I am also the law with a capital L. So I am going to think on this a little bit to try to come to a decision on how to proceed that best serves the requirements of justice. Okay?"

"Thank you, Sheriff," Cuddy said. "We are prepared to accept our punishment."

"Y'all need to understand that this decision is unrelated to whatever action your attorney decides to bring against Mr. Sargasso. I will not be a party to that unless I'm subpoenaed."

"We get that," Cassandra said.

"That's fine then," Billy said. "I am releasing you on your own recognizance and you will hear from me in due time, probably through your attorney. Please feel free to go."

"I'll walk you out to your car," Mickey Huntley said. When they reached the tan Celica, she said, "I don't want you to worry unnecessarily. Some sort of community service is the most likely outcome for this entire episode. Just go on about your lives and I will be in touch. As for your nephew's well-being, I will be back at your cousin's house within three days to interview him in preparation for a suit for damages against the brothers Sargasso and their various enterprises in civil court. I'd welcome seeing both of you there."

"We'll be there," they both said at once. "And thank you, Attorney Huntley," Cassandra added. "From the fullness of my heart."

"My friends call me Mickey," the lawyer said, and smiled.

We'd caught Coop on the phone with the message to get out of Carolina Beach before the CIA agent arrived to monitor him on the street where he lived. Coop had jumped in his car and met Stella and me as we were getting ready to leave Freddie's restaurant to head back to Bolivia.

"I hate leaving Jeff to fend off these Feds by himself," he said.

"He's a big boy," Stella said.

"Mickey's talked with him. She's going down to the boat at 7 tomorrow morning." I looked at my watch. "This morning, actually."

"Good. Because you know it's just a matter of time before they have a warrant on hand. If this was D.C., they'd already have one."

"The rural south has its charms," Stella said. Cooper smiled at her before he leaned in to kiss her. "It certainly does," he said.

Forty-five minutes later, we were all back at the Brunswick County Sheriff's Office in Bolivia. When we walked in, Sarah and Mickey were dozing on two cots that somebody had set up in Louise's outer office. In Billy's office, he and Louise and Eric Malanga were playing cards and drinking what smelled like bourbon. Billy was also eating a big bag of pork rinds.

"Daddy," Stella said, "those things'll kill you."

"How old's the first George Bush?" her father said.

"Ninety something," Louise said. "Why?"

"He ate a ton of these over the years," Billy said and winked at her. "I'm good for the next few decades."

"What's the game?" Coop asked.

"Poker," Eric said.

"Can a guy join in?"

"Have a seat, son," Billy said amiably. "The night's just getting started. The next shift don't start for another two hours."

When Attorney Mickey Huntley pulled in and parked on the far end of the parking lot that was closest to Jeff Davis's boat, the Portofino, it was 6:45 a.m. and the place resembled a three-ring circus. She had borrowed an unmarked car from Billy Conroy, so for the moment no one paid her any attention whatsoever. She took advantage of this and called her client.

"Hello," Jefferson said. He sounded wary.

"Did they board?" she asked.

"Not yet. I guess they're waitin' on a warrant."

"Okay, good. I'm right outside. I expect you know it's a madhouse out here. I've already spotted two local television stations. And it looks as though the entire police force from Carolina Beach is here, as well as some from neighboring jurisdictions. Not to mention dozens of curious onlookers. It may take me a few minutes to manage to climb aboard."

"I'm not going anywhere, Mick." Jeff Davis said.

Mickey Huntley hadn't walked ten feet toward the boat when she was spotted by two reporters who started walking to meet her, their microphones at the ready.

"What's going on, Attorney Huntley?" reporter number one asked. Mickey saw the camera rolling. "My client is being harassed by a federal agency about a matter he has no involvement in and of which he has no pertinent knowledge," Mickey said.

"A federal agency?" reporter number two said. The cameras kept rolling. "Which one?"

"My understanding is the CIA. Beyond that, I am unable to comment."

A summer law enforcement officer from a nearby community noticed the reporters interviewing a woman and moved to break it up. His instructions had been clear: this is a serious federal matter that must be dealt with quietly as well as judiciously. The police couldn't exactly bar the press or the crowd but they could contain it.

"Break it up," the young summer lawman said gruffly.

"Break what up?" Mickey Huntley asked. "Am I to understand that the First Amendment has been revoked?"

"What?" the cop said.

"It's called freedom of speech," one of the reporters said.

"And freedom of the press," the other reporter said.

"Our orders are to contain and limit," the young policeman said. "I follow orders." He drew his stun gun. "Break it up, now."

"You can't just order us…" reporter one started to say, as he pointed his microphone at the cop. He stopped when the stun gun zapped him in the middle of his abdomen. He dropped to the ground like a sack of stones. His cameraman caught it all.

The second reporter screamed and dropped to her knees to help her colleague. When Beatrice Bush, who had been talking on the phone with the New Hanover County District Attorney, heard the scream she turned immediately to see what was happening.

What she saw was this: a light-skinned black woman was looking earnest and saying something to a young white law enforcement officer who was looking at her with a stun gun loose in his hand. A young black woman was on her knees holding a young white man who appeared to be having a seizure. Then, as Beatrice Bush began to run to this scene, she saw the black woman extend her hand toward the young white policeman who staggered back a bit and then shot the woman in the upper chest. The stun gun's force caused this woman to fall heavily on her back, where she grimaced once before losing consciousness. Both of the cameramen caught it all.

"Drop the stun gun you fucking jackass," Beatrice Bush screamed at the top of her lungs to the young cop. To Bart Clarkson she yelled, "Call 911. Get an EMT here immediately."

When she reached the scene, she glared at the cop, whose hands were shaking. "Get the hell out of my sight," she said. I am dealing with a bunch of fucking fools down here, she said to herself. "Is he breathing?" she asked the young woman holding the man who had been hit by the electric current.

"Yes," the woman said.

"Good. Keep talking to him. It might bring him around."

Then she looked at the woman on the ground and realized that she wasn't breathing.

Beatrice Bush dropped to her knees and began CPR. She had been at it for nearly three minutes when the EMT truck pulled into the parking lot. "Over here," she yelled. "Bring a defibrillator and oxygen. One man's breathing on his own. A woman isn't."

Thirty seconds later, two EMTs attached paddles to Mickey Huntley's chest and shocked her. There was no response. A second shock also yielded nothing. One EMT looked at the other.

"Hit her again," the woman said to the man. On the third attempt, the attorney's chest convulsed slightly and the fourth resulted in a restoration of breath, although it was ragged. The woman placed the oxygen mask on Mickey to force and regulate her breathing. "She's back," one of them said to Beatrice Bush. "You did good. How long was she out?"

"Three minutes," Beatrice said. Her arms ached and she could feel the sweat running down her body. She realized she was also nauseous. She swallowed repeatedly to keep from vomiting.

"You saved her life," the male EMT said.

"Do y'all know who she is?" It was Police Chief Charlie Gowdy of Carolina Beach who asked the question.

"No, I don't." Beatrice Bush managed.

"That's Mickey Huntley. Lotta regular folks say she's the best defense attorney in the entire state of North Carolina. Lotta law enforcement folks wish she'd consider relocatin' to another more liberal state like California." He was grinning at her as he was talking.

Beatrice Bush didn't know whether to laugh hysterically or cry uncontrollably. Instead, she turned away from the Police Chief and vomited into the sand.

CHAPTER THIRTY THREE

Bart Clarkson had detained the summer law enforcement officer and was talking with him on one of the Boardwalk benches. "What's your name?" he asked the guy.

"Andy White," the guy said. He was still shaking and heavy sweat had stained the armpits and run down both sleeves of his crisp white shirt. He kept rubbing his hands together and both his knees were jerking up and down as though he had to get to a restroom quickly or suffer an accident.

"You work here in Carolina Beach?" Clarkson inquired.

"No. I work for New Hanover County Sheriff's Office. I float," White answered. "I was in Monkey Junction on patrol when I got the call to come down here, help with crowd control. I don't even carry a real gun," he said imploringly. Clarkson heard the anguish is the guy's voice and wondered if he was about to cry.

"Son, you nearly killed a woman with a stun gun. Her condition is critical. Believe me that's a real gun. It just substitutes electricity for bullets. Didn't they tell you that when they trained you?"

"She reached at me," the guy said defensively. "She threatened me. I had to defend myself. I had to keep order. Those were my orders. I follow orders." By now his voice had risen enough that people were turning to look at the two of them.

"That woman was no threat to you," Clarkson said patiently. "She was an unarmed civilian trying to talk you down from the road you'd chosen to take when you tasered that reporter."

"She's Mickey Huntley, a local big shot defense lawyer, a cop who was standing nearby said. "I'd hate to be you right now, kiddo."

Bart Clarkson glared at the cop who looked completely unconcerned and shrugged his shoulders before he walked away.

"What's gonna happen to me," the young deputy said despairingly.

"There'll be an inquiry," Clarkson said, while he inwardly filed the identity of the tasered woman. He hoped he wouldn't have to be the one to identify her to Beatrice Bush. "The whole incident was caught on camera. It'll most likely hinge on what charges, if any, that reporter and Attorney Huntley choose to file against you. Or, if they don't file, what the Carolina Beach Police Department decides to do. Your sheriff will also be involved."

"Chief Gowdy took my badge and stun gun," the kid said. "I guess I'm on leave pending the outcome. My mother'll kill me, she finds out."

"If your mother doesn't, I ought to," Beatrice Bush said emphatically as she returned from the restroom where she'd washed the remains of her early morning breakfast throw up off her face.

The summer deputy heard the fury in her voice and tried to stop himself but couldn't. He sat on that oceanfront bench in the bright August sunshine, put his face in his hands, and cried his young heart out.

Jefferson Davis had seen his friend and attorney get shot, had seen her fall, had watched Beatrice Bush applying CPR and finally had watched two emergency medical technicians revive her and place her, with an oxygen mask over her face, in their ambulance along with the news reporter, and speed away, headed for New Hanover Medical Center's Emergency Room.

His first reaction was shock. He could not wrap his head around what he had just seen. But his second reaction was the realization that nobody was paying him the slightest bit of attention. Now was his chance and he took it. He walked down the steps into his galley kitchen, walked on through to his bedroom and grabbed a grapple hook out of his closet. Then he went back on deck and around to the side of his boat that was facing the ocean rather than the shore, secured the hook to the railing and lowered himself into the water.

He swam strongly away from the marina and finally came ashore in front of Fins Island Buffet. He scooted up the short ladder to the outside deck and hurried past the popular restaurant. When he hit Lake Park Boulevard he turned right and walked quickly past the little stores and shops that dominated the busy roadway. A few minutes later, he hurried across Stone's Cut Bridge. At the first intersection he came to he turned right. Five minutes later, he knocked loudly on a door that was opened by Tallahassee Bodine.

"Y'all soaked to the skin, Jeff. What the hell's goin' on?"

"Who is it?" Junior yelled from the back of the house. "It ain't even seven thirty yet. I'm in my skivvies."

"It's Jefferson," Tally said, grabbing him and pulling him inside. "Bring me one of them big beach towels. The man's soakin' wet."

"I've got to make a call, Tally." Jeff Davis said. He was short of breath. "We've suffered a catastrophe."

"Say what?" Junior said. He was holding a huge towel which Tally took and wrapped around his early morning visitor's body. He was also wearing a pair of loud purple undershorts and a tee shirt that read "I'll Sleep When I'm Dead. Maybe."

"Sit down, Jefferson, catch your breath. Catastrophe, huh? Did the boat sink or did somebody die?" Tally was easing Jeff into one of the living room chairs when he said this.

Jefferson Davis's eyes suddenly filled with tears. They flowed down his face and all over his neck and chest. Tally and Junior were mortified. Jeff wasn't making a sound. He was just sitting there looking at Tally.

"Jesus, Tally," Junior said softly. "Go get one of the phones. I'll brew some coffee." To Jeff he said, "Y'all just take as much time as you need. No need for hurryin'. Tally and me will be right here for as long as it takes. Don't you worry 'bout that one little bit, Jefferson."

As Tallahassee Bodine was reentering the living room and Junior was in the kitchen making coffee, Jefferson Davis wiped his face, cleared his throat, and said, "A dumb cop shot Mickey Huntley real close up with a stun gun. I saw her fall and I don't know whether she's alive or dead."

The loud crash that emanated from the kitchen was followed by a curse from Junior as a bunch of water ran across the old planks and headed for the living room. He kicked the coffee pot clear across the room until it struck the front door.

Tally paid no attention. He walked over to Jeff, handed him the phone, sat across from him in the other living room chair and said, "Make your call. We'll talk after."

Jeff Davis felt the tears swarm his eyes and start to fall again. He kept seeing Mickey Huntley trying to reason with the cop, kept seeing her reach for the stun gun and kept hearing it go off and seeing her fall. "I can't, Tally. Call Billy Conroy's office. They're all there."

Tallahassee Bodine looked at Junior Fisk who was handing a bunch of Kleenex to Jeff. Junior nodded at him.

"Okay then," Tally said. As he dialed the number he was hoping Cash or Stella would answer the phone but he knew it wasn't likely.

"Brunswick County Sheriff's Office. How may I help you?" a cheerful female voice said.

"This here is Tallahassee Bodine, my own self," Tally said to her. "I need to speak with Cash or Stella. They still there?"

"Just a moment, Mr. Bodine," Louise Dickson said.

"Thank you," he said.

"What's up, Tally?" Cash Delaney said. "The kid move into the warehouse?"

Tally cleared his throat. "I got Jefferson here in my living room, looks like he swum here from his mooring. He can't talk good right now but we got us a doozy of a mess. Some cop shot Mickey with a stun gun and we ain't got no idea whether she's livin' or not. Jeff's a sight. We need y'all do somethin' quick."

He heard nothing but silence until he was forced to say, "Cash? Y'all still there?"

"I'm here," she said. "Where do you figure? New Hanover?"

Tally knew she was being cryptic which suggested that Sarah was nearby listening in. "I'd be puttin' money on it," he said. "My guess about an hour ago. If y'all are goin' there shortly, keep us informed. I expect Jeff'd love to see you. His heart's hurt bad."

"Hold the fort, Tally," Cash Delaney said. "I'll be in touch. And Tally, take good care of him. Believe it or not, he's a very sensitive guy."

"Yes ma'am. I know."

When Cash Delaney hung up the phone she was looking at Louise Dickson who noticed that she'd lost all coloring in her face. "You see a ghost, Cash?" Louise said. "You're white as a sheet."

"What was that all about?" Sarah Ehrenson asked. "Who were you talking to?"

"Tally," Cash said. "Jefferson swam from his boat to Tally's house."

"Why would he do that? He knew Mickey was on the way," Sarah said.

"Sarah, please sit down," Cash said.

"I don't want to sit down," Sarah said firmly. "I want an answer to my question."

"There's no good way to say this, Sarah. Mickey's been shot by a cop with a stun gun. She's been taken to New Hanover Medical Center for treatment. At the moment her condition's unknown."

Sarah Ehrenson laughed out loud. "Is this your idea of gallows humor," she said to her oldest friend. Cash Delaney looked at her. "Stun gun, indeed."

"It's not a joke, Sarah," she said quietly. "Mickey's fighting for her life."

Stella Conroy, who had been listening to this exchange from the door of her father's office, saw it first. Sarah's knees buckled. As she began to fall, Stella reached and put her arms around her waist and eased her over to a chair in front of Louise Dickson's desk. Louise ran to grab a cold washcloth. Sarah Ehrenson had fainted.

"Daddy'll drive us," Stella said. "He will most assuredly use the siren."

"We've got to revive Sarah," Cash said. "If we left her here, she'd walk to the hospital if she had to, never mind that it's sixty miles away."

"Here," said Louise. "This washcloth's ice cold. She'll come around."

"Will you call daddy?" Stella said to her. "Tell him to get a move on. It'll still take us a good hour to get to New Hanover even if we use the siren."

CHAPTER THIRTY FOUR

The Doctor at New Hanover Medical Center knew exactly who he was treating when they wheeled Mickey Huntley into the emergency room. The feisty attorney had saved his son from a life as a felon when she'd gotten a not-guilty verdict on a case of robbery that police had arrested the young man for. The doctor's gratitude was about to speak for itself.

"Status," he said to the two EMTs.

"She was unresponsive for three minutes," the female technician said. "but CPR was continually applied until we arrived with the defibrillator. It took four jolts to bring her back. She remains on oxygen. We didn't dare risk she'd breathe on her own."

"Thank you," the Doctor said. "Ordering," he called to a nurse standing by. "I need chest x-rays stat. We're looking for broken, cracked, or dislocated ribs. Anything that could impair her breathing. I also want blood work. Are her oxygen levels stable? Is there a dangerous accumulation of CO_2? How are her electrolytes? I need it yesterday."

"Yes, doctor," the emergency room nurse said. She'd never heard him so willing to share what he was looking for. She wondered idly who this woman was.

When the bloodwork was drawn and analyzed, it showed an oxygen level of 90%. This concerned the Doctor. If it dropped further, she'd be in crisis. But considering that she'd been unresponsive for three minutes, he said to the nurse, "Monitor her oxygen levels every fifteen minutes. It needs to go up to at least 95% for me to be happy."

When he looked at the x-rays, he saw two broken ribs. These could be tricky. Motion must be restricted along with a great deal of rest and sleep. At the moment, his primary concern was her breathing so he was disinclined to restrict her chest.

"Let's get her to a single room now. Let's make her as immobile as possible without using chest restraints. I'll be along in a few minutes to see if she'll breathe on her own. Continue the intravenous glucose until she wakes up, and add the electrolytes and monitor them every twelve hours until further notice. Her levels are low across the board. Thank you."

A half hour later, the doctor walked from Mickey Huntley's room back to the waiting room in emergency.

"Is anyone here waiting for an update on Attorney Huntley?" he asked.

Nearly everyone in the room said yes. A striking redheaded woman, who looked to be suffering, said simply, "I need to see her now."

"You are..." the doctor said.

"Sarah's her life partner," Cash Delaney said.

"So you're not related," the doctor, whose name tag read Dr. Stevens, said.

"North Carolina is currently not a welcoming state when it comes to diversity, I know; but please let me see her," Sarah said bluntly.

Doctor Stevens smiled. "Well, I'm not the state," he said. "If a few of your friends want to accompany you, that's fine with me. Mickey's breathing on her own but she's still unconscious. She has two broken ribs which I will treat when she wakes up. Right now, I'm monitoring her oxygen levels which have risen from 90% to 94%. Her outlook for a full recovery is fair to good but is, of course, dependent on her waking up. Any recovery will take time. And knowing Mickey that will be a challenge for you and your friends, Sarah. She's a genuine whirlwind. But she'll need a great deal of rest, sleep, and peace and quiet."

The doctor's reference to his patient as Mickey caught Cash Delaney's ear.

"So you know Attorney Huntley," she said.

"I do," he said. "Of course a lot of people in this area know her. In my case, she saved my son from a prison sentence."

Sarah had pulled a chair up to the side of the hospital bed closest to the door and she'd taken Mickey's right hand in both of hers and was rubbing it and speaking quietly to her. When she overheard the doctor's words about his son, she looked up at him.

"Of course," she said evenly. "You're Bradford Stevens. Mickey often spoke of you during the trial."

"Your partner never wavered in her belief that my son was innocent," he said. "And she'd often tell me that she would prove it. And she did. I couldn't be more grateful to her if I tried. Leonard's now a sophomore at Howard University. He's pre-law. He told me last week he was going to see if he could clerk with Mickey once he's started law school. I hope he can."

Billy Conroy and Cooper Grey were sitting in the waiting room attached to emergency when Beatrice Bush walked in with Agent Bart Clarkson and looked around. When she spotted the sheriff and Grey she walked over to them.

"How is she?" she said to the sheriff.

"Unconscious," Billy said tersely.

"Are they calling it a coma?"

"I don't know what the hell they're callin' it, Special Agent Bush. But I know what I'm callin' it and that is one hellacious fucking screw up, which is something you've been deliverin' to our doorstep ever since you and your gang of Keystones arrived on our turf. Y'all had so much as a lick of sense you'd hightail it back to your inner sanctum in Maryland or Virginia or wherever y'all come from and forget you was ever here. We're quite capable of cleanin' up after y'all."

"We're here on serious business, Sheriff Conroy, involving the national security of your country," Bart Clarkson said evenly.

Cooper Grey chuckled. "You're here on serious CYA business and a lot of people know it."

"What the hell are you talking about," Beatrice Bush said. Her jaw was flexing rapidly and it was clear she was attempting to control her temper.

"You think just because we're small town law enforcement officers we're stupid?" the sheriff asked her.

"I never said that and you know it."

"Maybe not to me. But how 'bout Haskell Shorter? Y'all think your treatment of him and his men went over well? And that don't even begin to equal how y'all are mistreatin' a good man used to work for you. Why aren't y'all mortified by your behavior?"

Sheriff Billy Conroy's question hung in the air like a live hand grenade. Nobody said a word for what seemed like an hour but was actually just a couple of minutes.

"Let's go check on Mickey, Billy" Cooper Grey finally said. "See how she's doing. See if the girls need anything."

"Good idea," the sheriff said.

When they'd left the room, Bart Clarkson turned to look at Beatrice Bush. Her face was bright red. "What now, Bea?" was all he said.

She didn't answer him for a while. Finally, she said very slowly and deliberately, "I don't know. I have to think. Get me out of here before I break something."

––––––––––––––––

Eric Malanga was watching the news and eating scrambled eggs with cheese, wheat bread toast with butter and raspberry jam, a half dozen pork sausage links and a huge mug of black coffee. He'd slept better than he had in a long while and he felt safer than he had in years. And I'm in a jail cell, he thought to himself. The irony made him happy.

Louise Dickson approached his cell and unlocked it. "Might as well come on out when you're through with breakfast," she said. "Stretch your legs. If y'all want something to do, Billy needs some help with the yard out back. He loves to look out his picture window at the garden but he's not so good at pruning and raking and stuff. Still he's got a pair of cardinals he loves that have lived there for years so the space is important to him."

"That's right up my alley," Eric said. "I'll be happy to help him out."

"Are you a gardener?" Louise asked.

"Well, not really. I'm a nature lover, I guess you'd say. I find a lot of peace being among the woods and rivers and wild fields. And I love to identify the flowers and watch the birds. I walked to the Green Swamp one day a few months ago and got giddy from breathing the air and basking in the beauty of the place. The wild orchids were breathtaking. I might have made it my home if it wasn't so dangerous. I'd be no match for the copperheads or rattlesnakes or alligators who do make it home. I'd be loath to kill any of them while any one of them wouldn't hesitate to make me their dinner." Then he grinned.

This man is charming, Louise Dickson thought to herself. To Eric she said, "Okay then. See you in a bit."

"Yes ma'am you will," he said and went back to finishing his breakfast.

"Your father did us all a favor, Stella," I said to my partner. We were standing in the hallway outside Mickey Huntley's hospital room where Stella had rushed after her father told us about his encounter with Beatrice Bush and her agent.

"How in the hell do y'all figure that?" she asked, wide-eyed.

"He put the Feds on notice. Keep investigating and roiling the waters, and there'll be big consequences to pay including the exposure of a massive cover-up of a decorated marine's death, not to mention the under-the-radar search to 'terminate' an innocent man."

"And y'all think that'll rattle Agent Bush?" she scoffed.

"Yes, I do. And if Mickey could speak, I think she'd agree with me. Special Agent Bush is now firmly ensconced between a rock and a hard place."

"Well, I reckon we'll find out soon enough if what you think is true," Stella said a bit more evenly.

"Yes, I'm certain we will." I said.

Sheriff Wayne Pinckney of New Hanover County was furious. But his young summer deputy wasn't his only target.

"If these yahoo feds needed an adversary they couldn't have picked a fiercer one than Mickey Huntley, Howdy" he said. He was talking on the phone to Chief Charlie "Howdy" Gowdy in Carolina Beach. "I talked with her a few days ago. She wasn't even aware they were scouring this whole area looking for some AWOL marine. Now that she is, in spades, look out. How is she, by the way? Have you heard?"

"Ain't heard a thing," Sheriff Gowdy said. "But she was dead for at least three minutes before they revived her."

"No kidding. That could turn out to be problematic."

"Speaking of problematic, I got your quick-draw McGraw in my conference room fretting himself to death. I took his badge and stun gun. What do you want me to do with him?"

"Are you planning on charges?"

"I'm waiting to hear from those he injured," Sheriff Gowdy said. "The reporter's doing good. I expect to interview him tomorrow at New Hanover. Mickey's another story entirely."

"Well, send him on his way to me," Sheriff Pinckney said. "I'll ground him for good. It's for sure he'll never work in law enforcement again regardless of how this travesty pans out."

"If Mickey Huntley dies," Charlie Gowdy said, "he won't be workin' anywhere for quite a while outside of four prison walls.

CHAPTER THIRTY FIVE

Stella, Coop, Billy and I left the hospital together. We were all still riding in Billy's police cruiser, but without Sarah this time. Mickey was still in a coma and Sarah had told me she wasn't leaving her side until Mickey woke up. She had also asked me to bring her books she'd decided to read to Mickey. Sarah insisted that Mickey would hear her. I tended to believe her.

The list included "My Life on the Road"; "A Room of One's Own"; "Sexual Politics"; "Bossypants"; "What Happened"; "The Wide Sargasso Sea"; "The Round House"; and "Diving Into the Wreck." Sarah said she wanted them no later than tomorrow evening. Until then, she was reading from a book entitled "Playing in the Dark: Whiteness and the Literary Imagination." One of Mickey's nurses had found it for her in the hospital library, which was stocked with donations from grateful patrons.

"Do I go to the public library?" I asked. I figured Sarah must have decided that Mickey would be out for a couple of months with the size of this list. I did not, however, share this thought with Sarah. So far, she was coping with this disaster very well and I didn't intend to rock that boat one tiny bit.

"No. Go to Two Sisters Bookery in downtown Wilmington. If

they don't have a couple of them then go to the main library. And Cash, bring me a suitcase of clothes. I can't wear what I now have on forever."

"Okay," I said. "I'll see you tomorrow evening. Try to take care of yourself, Sarah. Mick's going to need you to be at your best when she wakes up."

"Don't worry. I will be whether I am or not," my best friend said.

Billy Conroy dropped me off at Tallahassee's a half hour after I'd last spoken with Sarah.

"Let us know if y'all need anything," Stella said. "Coop and I are only a phone call away."

"You know I'll take you up on that. And Stella, I'll call you later. We'll need to powwow early tomorrow."

"I am plannin' on joinin' y'all at that particular powwow," Billy Conroy said. "I can most likely finish the case regarding the incidents at Sargasso Vineyards in a way that would be satisfactory to Mickey. Shame is as good a motivator as guilt to some folks."

"We'll see you then," I said as I exited the car.

When I knocked on the big front door of the splendid old Sawtelle house, it opened immediately.

"Cash," Tallahassee Bodine said urgently. "How is she doin'?" Then he hugged me for a good sixty seconds. Over his shoulder I could see Junior looking worried and ringing his hands. At that moment, I did not think it possible that I could love these two unlikely friends any more than I already did.

"Jeff's sleeping," Junior said quietly when Tally released me. "He was a true pitiful mess when he got here earlier. He nearly fell asleep in a living room chair. So bring us up to date. Mickey gonna be okay?"

"She's still unconscious," I said. "Her doctor is optimistic."

"Well now, that's good news, ain't it?" Junior said.

"Is Miss Sarah with her?" Tally asked.

"Yes," I said. "She's there for as long as Mickey is."

"That's fine then," Tally said. "Mickey is restin'. She know Miss Sarah is there. She is just takin' her time getting' back to business. And that is a good thing."

"You look a bit peaked, Cash. You hungry?" Junior asked. The minute he said that I knew I was starving.

"Yes," I said. "Very."

"We got shrimp and grits, blueberry cobbler, Tally's righteous coleslaw, and my award-winning milk punch," Junior said.

I felt my mouth start to water. Five minutes later I was served.

I stayed at Tally's until seven o'clock that evening. That's when Jefferson woke up, ate a shrimp po' boy, and took a shower. Tally drove us back to my rented home on Beach House Lane. Jeff and I spent a quiet evening listening to music and talking about what had happened and what we hoped would happen next. True to his nature, Jeff tended to blame himself for Mickey's current condition.

"I should have just let them board," he said at least three times in the span of a half hour.

"Was that the advice Mickey gave you?" I responded each time.

"I shouldn't have even asked her advice," he said argumentatively.

"So now you're your own lawyer," I retorted. "You know what they say: you've got a fool for a client."

"Do y'all ever just give in and agree with a guy?" he said sharply. I knew he wasn't mad at me. He was mad at himself.

"Not when the guy is wrong," I said sweetly. "And baby cakes, you are dead wrong on this one."

We had opened up the sleep sofa in the great room after a while and this is the song we fell asleep to when the hour was nearly midnight. The great Dinah Washington had recorded it in 1954 and it seemed to capture the totality of our current situation perfectly.

They heard the breeze in the trees
Singing weird melodies
And they made that
The start of the blues.

And from a jail came the wail
Of a down hearted frail,
And they played that
As part of the blues.

From a whippoorwill high on a hill,
They took a new note,
Pushed it through a horn
'til it was born into a blue note.

And then they nursed it, rehearsed it,
And gave out the news
That the south land
Gave birth to the blues.

When I woke up the next morning, Jeff had gone but he'd left a note. "I love you more than I love my life," he'd written. "And I love, love, love my life. Thank you for loving me back."

I have to admit, he's easy to love.

CHAPTER THIRTY SIX

"I'm goin' over to Sargasso's place as soon as I leave here," Billy Conroy said to Stella and me. "Were you the one ask Tallahassee Bodine to call me yesterday?" he said, looking at me.

"Yep. I wanted you to know about Anthony Sargasso's new laboratory in one of Big Daddy's renovated rental properties."

"Big Daddy of all people. Well, is the lab up and runnin'?" the Sheriff asked.

"Will be as of today," Stella said. "So we're hopin' to hell y'all can appeal to Anthony's sense of responsibility over his brother's indifference to the dangers of his concoctions. The one time Cash and I talked with him Anthony seemed to genuinely care about being an upstanding member of his community."

"Are you two gonna tackle the Feds?"

"We're going to think about how to proceed," I said.

"Maybe Mickey'll wake up sooner rather than later," Stella said.

"And maybe not," her father said. "The leverage is with y'all right now, Stella. Use it wisely, of course. But for Christ's sake use it."

"Not to worry, Billy," I said. "We will."

"And if your argument needs butressin', you for damn sure know who to call."

"That we do," his daughter said.

It was seven o'clock in the morning and Darius Millar looked as though he was going into shock. The nurse who was in the room switching the intravenous glucose drip that was providing nourishment to Mickey Huntley noticed his eyes begin to glaze over. He was standing at the foot of Mickey's hospital bed. If he fell over, he'd fall right on her.

"Please sit down in this chair by the window," she said to him. He didn't move an inch.

"Sir," she said in a louder voice. Still nothing.

Sarah Ehrenson walked out of the bathroom. She'd showered and changed her clothes. Cash had had her suitcase delivered by taxi late last night. A pleasant man named Art had told her the books would be delivered by five o'clock this evening.

"Your friend is in shock," the nurse said to Sarah. "Get him away from her. Otherwise he could fall right over on top of her. That chair by the window is good."

"Darius," Sarah said. He jerked his head to look at her. "I want you to go sit in that chair over there. Okay?" He nodded. But he didn't move.

"Jesus Christ, Darius. If you fall face first and hurt Mickey, I swear I'll never forgive you," she said. "Snap the hell out of your shock this very second and go sit down in that chair."

That did the trick. He sat in the specified chair. "Who did you say shot her?" he asked vaguely. "Where are the bandages?"

"I didn't say and there aren't any bandages yet," Sarah said. "She was shot by a sheriff's deputy with a stun gun at very close range. She has two broken ribs and she didn't breathe for three minutes. Two EMTS revived her after four shocks from a defibrillator. So here we are."

"Where was she shot?" he asked. "Last I knew, y'all were going to Ivanhoe."

"The CIA had impounded Jefferson's boat. She was responding to his call. We had left Ivanhoe and were all at the Brunswick County Sheriff's Office."

"The Feds shot Mickey?" he said incredulously.

"No," Sarah said emphatically. "A summer intern out of New Hanover County Sheriff's Office shot her. Can you please for heaven's sake focus!"

"I guess I never really thought of Mickey as being vulnerable," Darius said slowly. "Why doesn't she just wake up?" He sounded wistful, the way a child might when faced with a situation beyond his control.

"She'll wake up when she's ready to," Sarah said. "Meanwhile, I need your help. Can you please, please focus?"

"Of course I can," Darius said off handedly. He followed this perfectly logical response with a perfect non sequitur. "Should I talk to her? Can she hear me?"

Sarah Ehrenson debated whether to slap him hard across the face but decided instead to say, "I need you to bring me all of Mickey's notes in the Eric Malanga file. Do you know where it is?"

"Of course I do. I filed it," he said. He was still staring at Mickey.

"What did I just ask you to do, Darius?" Sarah said to him. He made no effort to respond.

The nurse, meanwhile, wanted to begin another part of her

morning ritual, which included bedding changes and catheter changes as well.

"Please step out of the room," she said to Sarah. "Please take Mr. Millar with you."

"Of course," Sarah said. She walked over to Darius and took his arm. "We can talk in the hallway, Darius."

Once in the hallway, Darius quickly regained his focus. "You need that Malanga file," he said to Sarah. "I'll go to the office right away. I should be able to get it to you in less than an hour. Call me with any news. And if Boss wakes up tell her the office is covered and there's nothing for her to fret about. I'll contact the ACLU about that amicus brief." Then he hugged Sarah, and as he turned to go he said to her, "Y'all take care of both of you, Miss Sarah."

Sarah smiled. "I will," she said. "And Darius, you will probably have a visit from the CIA, perhaps as soon as today. You don't know anything."

He's never seen Mickey in physical danger before, she thought to herself as he hurried down the hallway. Mickey's vulnerability scares him to death.

"I hear tell your brother's moved his laboratory," Sheriff Billy Conroy said to Paul Sargasso. The two men were standing in one of the rows of cabernet grapes that Sargasso grew and bottled for his own wine cellar. Paul was fussing because he'd lost a good picker so he was doing some of the picking himself. His manager was helping.

"I can't stop to talk with you right now, Sheriff. My designated picker up and quit without as much as a word to anybody. Didn't even collect the pay he had coming. So now it's up to me and Moody to gather these grapes before they rot."

Right now that picker is watching your brother move into his new digs, Billy thought to himself. To Sargasso he said, "Are y'all aware his new lab's in an old but newly renovated building that's owned by the biggest drug dealer on Wilmington's north side?"

"That's a lie," Paul Sargasso said. "My brother doesn't know any drug dealers."

"He knows Big Daddy Washington," the Sheriff said. "He's the Kingpin of the soft and hard drug trade in the city. Has been for years. Your brother signed his lease with Big Daddy this morning."

Paul Sargasso put his basket of grapes on the ground. Then he straightened up, untied and removed his sweatband, used it to wipe his face and neck and said to his manager, "Will you take over for a while, Moody?"

"Yessir," Moody said.

"Let's talk in my office in the barn, Sheriff Conroy. It's much more private."

"That is an excellent idea," Billy Conroy said.

Paul Sargasso was wondering whether or not he could still trust his brother to tell him the truth. Anthony had told him he was signing a lease today with a gentleman named Maurice Washington. However, he had neglected to mention anything about the gentleman's involvement in the distribution and sale of illegal drugs.

Deputy Lloyd Harris was perched on a corner of Louise Dickson's desk looking through the recent arrest files. Louise was busy typing something that looked like an accident report.

"Who's the guy workin' in the garden?" he asked her.

"What?" she said. The typing ceased for the moment.

"That guy outside pruning the rose bushes," Harris said. "Who is he?"

"Billy's helper," she said. "You know perfectly well that Billy himself hates gardening. But he loves his garden."

"Billy's helper," Harris said. "That's his name?"

The voice of the 911 operator broke into this potentially dicey conversation. "Three alarm fire at 1223 Sanders Road, Southport. Possible three people trapped inside. Arson suspected. Please respond. Over."

Lloyd Harris jumped off the desk and ran outside to his patrol car. His partner was already in it. "Deputy Harris and Deputy Rivenbark responding," Louise Dickson said. "Over and out."

CHAPTER THIRTY SEVEN

Special Agent Beatrice Bush was doing a lot of listening, interspersed with a lot of 'Yessirs' as her boss at the CIA, Director of Internal Affairs Roland Bishop, expressed his complete and utter dissatisfaction with the way her special investigation had proceeded thus far.

"At this point, the entire situation is untenable," he said.

"Yessir," she said.

"What do you intend to do next?" he asked.

"I'm seeking your guidance," she said evenly. Inwardly, she was seething. And her fury was directed at everyone and everything she had encountered in what she had decided was one of the most ridiculous hidebound areas on the face of the earth.

"My guidance!" he said sarcastically. "You have no idea where Eric Malanga is and you are unlikely to ever find out; you have no idea if he is actually responsible or even proximately responsible for Woody's death; you covered up the unfortunate murder of an active duty marine by two trigger-happy sheriff's deputies, and in so doing blamed that death on the man you were sent to locate and retire; you impounded a yacht that is owned by a man with no direct involvement in your mission and, unbelievably, that action has resulted in the possible demise but at the very least critical injury of one of North Carolina's most well-respected and prestigious defense attorneys. Did I miss anything, Special Agent Bush?"

"Not really," she said dejectedly. But I am really going to miss my lovely townhouse in D.C. when you ship me off to the boonies of Hell, Michigan or Noodle, Texas, she thought to herself.

"The only sane thing left for you to do is enter into binding agreements with all affected agencies and individuals that state they will maintain silence regarding this entire mess. Call it a federal non-disclosure agreement, have everyone affected sign one, make the penalty for ignoring it severe and have it drawn up by one of our in house lawyers. Do it ASAP and keep me informed. Can you manage that much, Special Agent Bush?"

"Yessir," she said. Roland Bishop didn't hear that last obsequity. He had hung up.

Bart Clarkson had remained out of earshot on the terrace of the hotel suite during this call. He didn't want to hear more than whatever Beatrice Bush chose to tell him about it because he honestly thought she'd done as well as anyone could have in directing this mission. He'd known from the start it would be difficult. He'd never dreamed they would run into the kind of interference they did, and every time they turned around. He still wasn't exactly sure what happened. And there was no one in particular to blame. The only thing that seemed to be true to him was that they'd simply been outplayed, which is precisely what FBI Agent David Keating had warned them might well happen.

"Is it noon?" Bea said to him. He jumped a bit at the sound of her voice. He hadn't heard her coming. He looked at his watch. "It's one-thirty, actually." he said. "Why?"

"I want a gin and tonic," she said. "Feel free to join me."

"Think that's a good idea?" he asked.

"I wouldn't recognize a good idea if it hit me upside the head," she said.

"You know, Bea, I've been thinking about those two seemingly average private investigators. They're not average. They're damned good at what they do. But one sounds like a red neck and the other one barely speaks, at least when they're confronted with someone they consider adversarial. So it's easy to underestimate them. And we probably did right from the start."

"Are you trying to make me feel better?" she said. "Or are you fixing me a drink." He had rarely heard her so subdued.

"Both, I guess," he said, and walked back into the living room.

"At the moment, about the only thing that would make me feel better is a guarantee of a completely painless way to commit suicide," Beatrice Bush said. Bart Clarkson couldn't tell if she was kidding or not.

"I just spoke with Billy," Louise Dickson said to Eric Malanga. "He wants me to move you to his house. Lloyd Harris was grilling me this morning about who you are."

"That sounds risky for the sheriff," Eric said. He was back resting in his cell after spending two hours working in the sheriff's garden. He had tuned in to CNN, where a discussion was growing heated over the economic disaster that might materialize if a trade war broke out with China. The subtext seemed to include whether or not anybody or anything could muzzle the current president. He muted the audio.

"It's no bigger a risk than keeping you here," Louise said. "And

Billy's home is his castle. No one ever visits him unannounced, including his daughter and me. So actually it's the safest place for you."

"Well, if you're sure," he said.

"I'm sure and we'd best hurry. I don't want you still here when Lloyd gets back from that fire he was called out to this morning."

"I'm ready," he said to her, flipping the television off.

"Good. Let's go."

———————————

Stella and I had spent the day organizing the case we intended to present to Special Agent Beatrice Bush that would ultimately include amnesty for Eric Malanga. We had gathered witness statements from the various parties with knowledge of his meeting with Woody Keats and Keats's subsequent behavior that had ultimately resulted in his accidental death. What we had decided to do next was interview three disparate parties who could bear witness to the CIA cover up of the death of the active duty marine: Sheriff Billy Conroy, who had confirmed it through a personal conversation with Haskell Shorter; Sheriff Shorter himself; and as unlikely as it sounds, Maurice Washington.

"Y'all think Big Daddy'll do it?" Stella said.

"I do," I said. His leverage with the FBI remains intact and he has no need of leverage with the CIA."

Then we decided to include Sheriff Shorter's testimony that Special Agent Beatrice Bush had ordered him to make no statement about what really happened when the marine was killed while she chose to frame an innocent man, Eric Malanga, for his death.

"If that won't do it, nothin' will," Stella said.

"That'll do it if it can be done. I just wish Mickey was awake. She knows how to write it in legalese, which always makes it sound terrifying," I said.

"Hell, it's terrifyin' in plain old English." Stella said, lighting a cigarette.

The office phone rang. "C& D Investigations," I said perfunctorily.

"Cash, it's Billy," the Sheriff said. "I am in the middle of serious negotiations with Paul Sargasso regardin' Cassandra's nephew, but I just got a call from Special Agent Bush. Have y'all reached out to her yet?"

"Not yet," I said. "We're still working on the proposal. We'll get to her in a few hours."

"No, don't call her," Billy said. "From what she said to me, she's gonna propose her own solution to this boondoggle and it sounds like we're gonna be very comfortable acceptin' what she has in mind."

"Are you serious? I said. Stella glanced up quickly when she heard the incredulity in my voice.

"I am deadly serious. Beatrice Bush is gonna throw in the towel, yell uncle at the top of her lungs, and toddle on back to Washington or wherever. Our part seems to be we sign off on a guarantee of silence about the whole stinkin' mess. Y'all should have no problem whatsoever with that."

"No kidding," I said. "Well, I certainly never saw this coming. Let me give Stella the news. Please keep us informed regarding Sargasso's intent."

"I'll do that," the Sheriff said.

"What was that all about?" Stella asked.

"Your father got a call from Special Agent Bush," I said.

"Apparently she wants a truce. He says she's going to return from whence she came as long as we sign non-disclosure agreements to maintain silence about this entire travesty."

"Where do I sign?" Stella said "Quick before she changes her mind."

"I wonder how many people she's going to ask to sign one," I said. "You and I both know there are quite a few people who know all about it whose identity she is unaware of."

"I do not feel that I'm under any obligation to share that information with her," Stella said. "It never hurts to have a backup plan when and if the CIA should decide to change its mind about Eric Malanga."

Sheriff Billy Conroy was exhausted when he returned to his office in Bolivia late in the afternoon. He plopped down in one of the two chairs in front of Louise Dickson's desk and sighed.

"Did y'all move Eric to my house?" he asked her.

"Hours ago," she said. "Where have you been? You look tired."

"I am tired," he said. "I pretended I was Mickey for most of the day."

"I wouldn't touch that with a fifty-foot pole, Billy," she said to him. "What happened?"

"Paul Sargasso called his lawyer in regardin' the damages both sides in this case have suffered," Billy said. "I did point out that they surely could not be considered equal."

"Were you able to agree on a suitable disposition?"

"I'm happy with it," the sheriff said. "I just hope Mickey'll give it a thumbs up when she hears about it."

"I'd like to hear about it now."

"I agreed to provide supervision of Cassandra and Cuddy while they replant the vines that they damaged or killed. I also agreed that they would provide a month's community service at that graveyard that's fallin' into itself on some of Sargasso's land. Sargasso says he'll pay Cassandra's nephew's surgeries up to $500,000.00 and he'll spring for six months' physical rehabilitation. This indemnifies him from prosecution if his brother's ever convicted of drug trafficking because of this situation."

"Billy, that is wonderful," Louise Dickson said sincerely.

"Y'all think Mickey'll be ok with it?" he asked.

"I think she'll be very proud of you and grateful to you," she said. "I know I am."

"Let's go get a bite, Louise. I am one famished man. Arm wrestlin' with lawyers is most assuredly not my cup of tea."

CHAPTER THIRTY EIGHT

Toward the end of what we all decided to call the "bush league affair," the woman whose last name we borrowed for our sobriquet did not dawdle. Within two days' time, those of us who were on an internal CIA list were asked to sign an agreement to remain silent about what had happened once federal agents had landed among us, although some of us would have added things to that list about which we would forever remain silent.

We were able to inquire about the status of Eric Malanga as it related to his connection to the CIA. We were told that although he remained a person of interest to the agency, they were no longer pursuing him for whatever purposes they had earlier held. Stella and I decoded that to mean they were not actively hunting for him but if he showed up at their headquarters he would still most likely disappear from the face of the earth.

And as suddenly as they had appeared, they were gone.

"I kinda miss old Bart Clarkson," Stella said to me one afternoon while we were busy working a corporate case. "He was at least fun in a hellish sort of way."

I grinned at her. "You just liked his looks," I said. "Admit it."

Instead of answering me, my partner lit a cigarette, took a deep drag, and then answered our loud landline telephone.

"Stella here," she said. Then she said, "Uh huh." She repeated that three more times. Finally she said, "Yeah, we know him. He mixes chemicals that make kids do stupid and dangerous things like try to fly. Why?"

She glanced at me and mouthed "Big Daddy." I nodded. "Y'all don't say," she said. "That's gotta hit you as one hellacious irony, Maurice. Uh huh. I don't doubt it for a minute. Well, next time call us. We'll do y'all a solid and run a background check." She hung up the phone and laughed out loud.

"The DEA, along with the FBI and the Wilmington Police raided Big Daddy's warehouse the Sargasso kid had rented and they're holding it as a crime scene. The kid and his assistant are in Wilmington City Jail pending arraignment on a whole list of charges. Big Daddy is big time pissed off."

"I bet," I said. "Why'd he call us?"

"One of his street snitches told him that daddy was providin' evidence that there was a badly injured teenager recoverin' from havin' ingested some of those chemicals. Big Daddy's always excelled at puttin' two and two together."

"I guess the Sargasso kid was still selling the concoction that crippled Cassandra's nephew. The DEA must have used its emergency powers to declare it illegal and then picked him up."

"Be my guess," Stella said. "Y'all gotta admit it's kinda sorta ironic big Daddy gets caught up in a big drug bust but isn't the guy who's arrested."

That evening Jeff and I drove to New Hanover Medical Center to relieve Sarah for a few hours. Darius had decided he was going to take her out to dinner and she'd agreed that a break would do her some good. Mickey's condition had continued to improve but she still had not wakened from her coma which was now going into its second week. Doctor Stevens was not overly concerned, but I was beginning to wonder what was going on. I had expected the lawyer to snap out of it after a few days. Mickey decided to prove me wrong.

Before she and Darius headed out, Sarah handed me a book. "I'm reading excerpts from "What Happened"," she said. "I left off right here."

"Okay," I said. I looked at the book. "Oh, this is Hillary Clinton."

"Yes. Mickey read it but I'm rereading it to her because she got so damned mad when she read it I'm hoping that anger returns and she wakes right up. Darius and I will be back by ten."

"We'll be here," Jeff said. "Take your time. Enjoy yourself."

When they'd gone, he said to me, "Would you like me to read to her? I don't mind."

"Nope," I said. "When I tell Sarah I'll do something I do it. You could, however, get us a couple cups of coffee, large. Maybe a few cookies, too."

"You got it," he said. "I'll be right back."

I settled in the chair next to Mickey's bedside and started to read. A few minutes later one of the evening nurses walked into the room and began to switch out Mickey's glucose drip. "Don't let me interrupt you," she said. "I'll just be a few minutes."

I nodded at her and continued to read. "After nine days of turmoil—nine days in which millions of Americans went to the polls to vote early—and just thirty-six hours before Election Day, Comey sent another letter announcing that the 'new' batch of emails wasn't really new and contained nothing to cause him to alter his months-old decision not to seek charges. Well, great. Too little, too…"

Mickey Huntley said suddenly "too damned late. If it were up to me I'd sue for breach of ethics." Then she opened her eyes. It startled the nurse so much she fell backwards against the wall of the room and the new glucose drip fell to the floor. My eyes must have been as wide open as a deer in the headlights.

"Mickey!" I said. My voice was full of amazement.

Another nurse ran into the room and looked at the scene. "I'll call Doctor Stevens," she said and quickly ran out of the room.

"I'm not exactly sure what's going on," Mickey said, "but I do know I am really very thirsty."

The discombobulated nurse regained her equilibrium. "You've been in a coma, Attorney Huntley. You were shot with a stun gun a while ago."

"Well, that I don't remember off hand," Mickey said. "Will somebody please get me something to drink?"

Just then, Jefferson returned to the room. "You woke up," he said gratefully. "Thank god."

"Perhaps you should be thanking Hillary Clinton," the nurse said shyly.

POSTSCRIPT

Two weeks after Mickey Huntley was discharged, she and Sarah were sitting in the sun outside our cottage on Beach House Lane when a tan Celica pulled into one of the parking spaces. Cassandra Quick and Eric Malanga got out of the compact and walked over to join them.

"You're looking well, Attorney Huntley," Eric said.

"Please call me Mickey," she said. Then she gestured for each of them to have a seat.

"How are you feeling?" Cassandra asked.

"Pretty well," Mickey said. "I'm still wrapped up tight with these damned bandages while my ribs knit but otherwise I'm good."

"She's quite cranky," Sarah said happily. "That tells me she's on the mend. Her doctor tells us she should be able to have the bandages removed by the end of the month."

"How about you," Mickey said to Eric. "What are you up to?" Eric Malanga looked at Cassandra Quick.

"Eric is helpin' me with some things," Cassandra said. "We are buildin' a ramp at my niece's for my nephew to use when his surgery's finished. Eric is going to supervise his rehabilitation once he's released from the hospital.

And we are getting ready to till up a plot of my ground for a winter crop of cabbage and potatoes and squash and we got some chickens from friends of ours and we bought one young rooster so we're swimmin' in fresh eggs. We brought along a pail full for you two."

"Are you staying with your sister?" Sarah asked Eric.

Again Eric looked at Cassandra.

"He's stayin' with me," Cassandra said. "It's a haul from Topsail to Elrod and he doesn't have a car. And, well, we like each other." She smiled while Eric blushed bright red.

"I think that's splendid," Sarah said.

"It surely does agree with me," said Cassandra. "He's a big help with housework. I'm not much of a cleaner and he's neat as a pin. He's takin' care of everything while I do my work at Sargasso's vineyards."

"My sister often visits," Eric said quietly. "She was over last weekend and brought a couple of grouper she'd caught. We grilled it outside. She's also agreed to help some of Cassie's friends with investments."

"He calls me Cassie," said Cassandra. "I'm getting used to it."

"Sarah often calls me Mick," Mickey Huntley said. "Because it's usually derogatory slang for an Irish person, it took a while, but I got used to it."

"You objected to it?" Sarah said. "Really? You never told me that."

"Love is a powerful arbiter," Mickey Huntley said. "And I am, after all, a lawyer. I ought to know."

ABOUT THE AUTHOR

Beverlee Hughes started this novel in 2014. Then she was interrupted...by politics, which still impinges on her time.

AUTHOR'S NOTE

My heartfelt thanks to the actual Brooke Malanga, who graciously allowed me to use her name in this novel. I hope she made it to Montana.